John Rankine

THE
RING OF GARAMAS

LONDON : DENNIS DOBSON

00689050

Printed in Great Britain by
Bristol Typesetting Co. Ltd., Bristol
ISBN 0 234 77676 5

F LETCHER reckoned it was none of his business. Sitting with his back to a plushy red reredos, he watched the developing scene through a long gilt mirror at the closed end of his alcove.

Dog eating dog. Let them get on with it.

He had never liked the Garamasians. Maybe only men like himself, who were actively engaged on a stint with the Galaxy's peacekeeping force, could see the folly of playing both ends against the middle. For the rest, Garamas was working a very smart operation; keeping out of commitment and running a high level economy at the expense of both sides.

Plumb on the frontiers of I.G.O. space, Garamas was courted by both the Inter Galactic Organization and the Outer Galactic Alliance. So far, its government had refused to come off the fence. I.G.O., respecting the processes of law, used diplomacy and trade as levers to keep her in their sphere of influence. O.G.A. suited the Garamasian national character which leaned to the military-style junta governments of that group. Historically, Garamas belonged with Lados, which although not one of the hard-core O.G.A. planets, had satellite status and binding treaty obligations.

Something was definitely in the wind. O.G.A. could be moving to a definitive trial of strength and Garamas was a natural spring board into I.G.O. space.

Secret police in any culture had a family look; but Fletcher saw the four who had moved quickly into the bistro as prototypes of the genre. Garamasian physical architecture was right for the illusion. They were tall, hitting the two-metre mark, narrow and high shouldered with long arms and legs. Heads balanced symmetrically on short necks, were almost perfect spheres. Eyes, which were lidless, seemed flat set, as though pasted on; black disks of polished obsidian. Head to foot in black, with calf-high, laced boots and yellow arm bands carrying the three intertwined rings of Garamas, they looked like vultures.

Except for the piped music, which was currently set for a sentimental ballad, out of key with events, the whole place had gone quiet. Two policemen had stationed themselves expertly where no one could pass. The other two were taking it slowly, one on either side of the aisle checking out the clientele.

Fletcher's own face was set bottom right of the composition like an inset on a scanner. It was a long, Indo-European job, heavily tanned from the last mission, left eyebrow given a quizzical twist by a thin, radiation burn. A hard face, with grey eyes that gave nothing away. His expression did not change, when pneumatic pressure built up against the back of his legs and a long slim hand appeared on the table top beside his own.

There was a quick-spreading pollen cloud of verbena, a muted sigh effort and a Garamasian citizen hauled herself out of the void to take the neighbour seat on his bench.

She was young. Not more than twenty at a guess, though estimates of age for other ethnic groups was liable to surprising error. The female of the Garamasian line was more sympathetic than the male. This one looked like a Raggedy-Ann doll, and was clearly working hard to fight back fear. Her left

6

hand, still clutching the table top, had picked up a small muscular tremble and she covered it with her right to make it behave.

It was a gesture that made more impact on Dag Fletcher than any number of words. At first, he had meant to play it out after the Garamasian pattern of neutrality. But any human being fighting fear needed an ally. He said 'Are they looking for you?'—using the basic speech-tone code which was the *lingua franca* of the galaxy.

The girl answered obliquely, anxious to save face before a stranger, speaking in English in a husky, vibrant voice. 'Do not think that I am afraid for myself. But I know my limitations. If I am taken, I shall be forced to talk. That will involve others. There is only one safe way.'

It was an open confession, that was dangerous enough in itself. But the ongoing action aimed to take the risk element out of it. The move to the end alcove had been made to gain time for a definite purpose. She stretched over, picked a tooth-edge steak knife from the cutlery rack and, without a pause, began to saw at the inside of her left wrist.

Fletcher had a split second to make a decision. A man or, in this case, a women, had a right to decide when the life situation was untenable. It was a choice he was prepared to make for himself. Indeed, every deep space operator, military or civilian, carried an oblivion capsule to make such a choice possible, when circumstance turned sour—a statistical possibility that they learned to live with.

But that was when human endeavour had gone to the limit and was still not enough. Here, there must be a chance for life. He grabbed for the knife and stopped its movement.

The nearest guard was two alcoves away, haranguing a countryman in high-pitched Garamasian.

Fletcher said, 'Your name. Quickly. Your name.'

7

'It is Yola. Please allow me to continue. You do not know what you are doing. Please.'

'I am Fletcher. Commander Fletcher, I.G.O. corvette *Terrapin*. You are attached to me as interpreter. Do you understand?'

It was unlikely that anyone on Garamas would know that *Terrapin* was a burned-out wreck on a cinder heap and that just now, waiting for a new posting, her one-time commander was in a limbo with no official status, until the enquiry court made the formal announcement that his conduct of the engagement had been free from negligence.

'It will not work.'

'It will work.'

Black disk eyes held his for a second, and he saw himself reflected there, in duplicate, as though he was trying to convince himself.

Yola drew down the cuff of her blue and white shirt to hide the raw cut and said heavily, 'I do not know why you should try to do this for me. But you do not understand the seriousness. If you fail, you will be implicated and I.G.O. will not help you. This is a neutral country.'

Fletcher stood up and shoved his hat on at a piratical angle. Male-Female relations on Garamas tended to be basic and brutal. Only pressure from I.G.O. had brought a measure of freedom to the women in the main centres. In up country areas, they still tended to be counted with oxen as useful to husbandry. Following the culture pattern, sure that he was heard by the guard at the nearer door, he said, curtly, 'Hurry Yola, I do not have all day to wait.'

Without checking that he was being followed, he walked straight for the exit.

He was a metre from the guard, before the man moved and could hear the girl's sandals flip-flopping behind him. He had banked on the impact of a uniform and unfamiliar rank insignia which could mean anything.

Certainly the I.G.O. shore-going rig was impressive, brilliant white, with a sun-burst blazon left of centre on the chest and green and gold rank tabs on the epaulettes.

Fletcher leaned on the Garamasian passion for neutrality. They would not go for a showdown with an I.G.O. official without serious reason. In this case, if they were looking for a Garamasian, it was obvious that no amount of disguise would turn him into an Earthman.

Face had to be saved, however. As he stepped aside, the guard shot out an arm to block the way for Yola.

Fletcher was round, in a turn that brought him face to face with the security man. He said harshly, 'What is it? What do you want with my interpreter?'

'Do you know this girl?'

Fletcher looked at her as though forced to acknowledge that a convenient piece of equipment had a separate entity and a name, a nice mime, lost to the boards.

'Of course. She has worked with me since my arrival a week ago. Now we are expected at a conference. Let her pass.'

At the same time, he took the extended arm in a double grip above and below the elbow and returned it to vertical.

Yola, no slouch at seizing an opportunity, went ahead. The door was two metres off. She could have been through. But she stopped and waited.

It saved the day. In the guard's book, any guilty party would have been out and away. Except for the high-handed action of the Earthman, there was no problem. He said, 'I will check with your organization. I hope, for your sake, it is as you say. You may go.'

Outside, Fletcher called an auto shuttle and dialled for the Space Centre; but it was not until they were in a screened interview room in the Earth Planet Consulate that he spoke again to Yola.

The Garamasienne said, 'You were very wise, Commander, all the auto shuttles are tapped. In fact, even to speak near them is to invite an eavesdropper. The monitors run a sampling service, you understand, four times out of five all would be well; but it is never safe. I must thank you for your help and now I will go. There is no longer any danger. If I had been questioned just then it would have been fatal. But now the group has had time to disperse.'

'Not so fast. That guard is going to check through. We have to fix your cover. I can do that; but you must leave your address and registration details for the record. I suppose you don't want to tell me what it was all about?'

'I regret that I cannot. You must understand that many others are involved. But be sure that I shall report your action. Perhaps it will be possible to repay. Who knows how the wheel of fortune may swing. Meanwhile, I will do as you say.'

Fletcher pushed over an ivorine memo tablet and Yola scribbled industriously in a round, feminine hand. But she made no query about the lay out. When the tablet was passed back, Fletcher saw that the detail was meticulously spaced for scanning by a computer. The girl was familiar with sophisticated equipment.

The detail told why. She was a final year student at the Kristinobyl Polytech. One of the few women to penetrate the thicket of higher education.

He said 'Fine. Now I think you should come back here each day for a little time to give the cover a chance. I expect to be on my way soon. But the next two or three days for sure. Ask for me at the desk.'

When she had gone, Fletcher talked to the Earth Consul.

Frank Yexby, soured by a ten year stint on Garamas, was

critical. 'You took a chance, there, Dag. If they'd picked you up for aiding and abetting, I couldn't have done a thing about it. You'd have been inside for God knows how long. They're touchy about interference. Do you know how many foreigners they have interned here? It'll surprise you. Intelligence reported over ten thousand at the last count. They even have a round dozen ships impounded at this time for minor breaches of the neutrality regulations. Usually they're cleared in a few weeks, but they've had two O.G.A. military units on ice for the last six months. Just to show impartiality. Though my guess on that, is that they don't mind having two Scotian frigates held here. Once the crews were back on board, they'd be in business. It's a counter-weight to I.G.O. patrol visits. I reckon Varley's playing a variant of that game with the corvette he left behind.'

'*Petrel*?'

'That's the one. Supposed to be held up for spares, but I have doubts. There's something brewing up here.'

'What's this girl been doing?'

'God knows. There's a whole raft of small political groups. Votes for women, more than likely. They get very emotional. Probably there was very little to it, but she'd worked herself into a death before dishonour state. You're lucky she didn't chain herself to your leg.'

'It's serious enough for her to be ready to kill herself.'

'They're a funny lot. I don't pretend to understand them. Half the time, you'd swear they hadn't a human emotion. Then something comes up and a character you'd believed was pig iron all through, turns out as neurotic as a flea. I can tell you, the present government is only in on sufferance. It's a coalition of moderates, represents a minority overall I would say. Given any external threat and the backwoodsmen would be in at full strength. Then there'd be a resurge of traditional

11

habits. Your friend Yola would be back pulling a plough before you could say universal suffrage.'

'Can't I.G.O. do anything about it?'

'It suits to let things ride. Garamas is a clearing house for all sorts of information. Too much pressure would give the extremists a lever on a national pride ticket. Don't worry. Human life has been with us a long time. You have to think in millenia. Not easy for the military mind.'

Dag Fletcher reckoned that he was getting training in it. Making his daily report visit to the I.G.O. complex, he got the stall he had been given for the last seven days. No posting through and the official report on *Terrapin* still not published.

That was an odd one. He went back in his mind over the session in Varley's command cabin on the squadron flagship *Europa*. There has been no suggestion that it was anything other than an open and shut case. There had been four officers on the board; Admiral P. J. Varley in the chair with Group Commander Frazer, captain of *Europa* beside him. Then Cameron, Commander of *Hawk* and Cooper, Commander of *Drake* both involved in the action. The decision to sacrifice *Terrapin* had been at squadron level. She had been damaged beyond repair in the engagement. Fletcher and the surviving members of his crew had been brought off by *Hawk* within minutes of the escalating power pack passing a point of no return.

At the Tribunal, there had been an air of simple formality. They all know the score. *Terrapin* had been spearhead in a complex and difficult manoeuvre, for the corvette screen that had intercepted a roving, free-lance cruiser, long a menace on the shipping lanes and brought her to bay, until *Europa* herself could come up with the final solution.

Ever sensitive to his rating in his own and other people's

estimate, Fletcher had been sure in this case that his handling of the corvette could not have been faulted. Cameron, Commander of *Hawk*, had said, 'Bloody marvellous, Dag. But I thought you were a goner for a sure thing. We'd never have held the bastard, if you hadn't gone in close. Varley ought to give you a medal. Which is not to say that you still won't get a raspberry.'

Well, maybe that was it. Now the detail was blurred and the action cold, he was less sure that he had done all he could to save the ship. A delayed raspberry might be filtering through the channels.

When it came, it took a form that he did not expect. The I.G.O. official pushed over the signal with a social smile, but there was a definite temperature drop in the plushy office.

The form of words was civil enough. 'It seems Commander, we are to have the pleasure of your company for some time yet. I am to inform you, if there are any local duties which you can carry out.'

The signal itself was brief enough. 'Commander D. Fletcher. Release of findings of tribunal on loss of *Terrapin* is postponed pending further enquiry. Await posting instructions in Kristinobyl.' It was signed by the Officer Commanding the Rim Task Force of which Varley's squadron was a part.

What had begun as a prudent exercise to regularize Yola's cover, was continuing because Fletcher was getting interested in the Garamasian scene. She knew the Kristinobyl that the tourist did not see and it gave him a new slant on the national character.

It was another proof of the basic truth that the longer you could defer judgement, the more likely it was to be accurate. But it also brought in another bit of philosophic lore in that the more sides of a question you see, the less likely you are to form any opinion at all.

Fletcher was used to making snap appraisals of groups that he saw briefly and would not see again. The silvery people of Fingalna were immediately sympathetic, the bulky jingoists of Sabazius were not. Maybe if he had done a study in depth, he would have found that the latter were way ahead on soul.

Here, he had been ready to write the planet off, while it caught up with his preconceived notions of a cultured state; but Yola opened his eyes.

Listening to voices and following the cut and thrust of argument, he began to see them as people in their own right and not as an odd variant of what the true flower of *homo sapiens* should be. Even by Earth standard, the women in Yola's circle had a certain kinky charm. Hands and feet were very slender and elegant. Hair was jet black, very fine with a shiny liquid flow when they moved. Dress was always plain and severe as a uniform as though they knew they were on sufferance in an all-male reservation; but perfume was an extension of personality. Every last one was her own alchemist, brewing up olfactory harmonies for the *noa noa*.

Technically, they were abreast of most planets on the Rim. One single feature would give them a niche in the hall of fame. For many years they had been using an unlimited power source which was brilliant in its simplicity.

A continuous land mass girdled the planet on its equatorial line. With incredible labour, a continuous conductor had been built to ring the globe smack on its zero latitude. Planet spin, combined with a daily drift of magnetic field back and forward across the line, generated more energy than could be used in the forseeable future, at a give-away price.

It was an exercise that had suited the national character. Ant-like labour gangs had toiled through deserts, lakes, moun-

14

tain ridges and every obstacle that an engineering project ever met.

Ironically, it had broken the government that conceived the plan and forced it through. A backlash reaction from the patient masses that had borne the heat of the day and suffered untold, unrecorded casualties had toppled the junta to put in a short-lived popular front.

This flowering of genius exhausted the tree. No comparable development followed in any field. Except for the paradox of having the cheapest power system in the galaxy Garamas remained three-fifths backward. Social organization trailed badly. It was a feudal system with neon-lit battlements and a power drive on the iron maiden.

Yola knew all about the Ring. Its administration absorbed half the graduates of the Polytech. She had specialized in science courses which would lead automatically to a junior post in the organization. There, she would be breaking new ground for the female faction.

One afternoon, she took him to see her department at the Polytech. It was dominated by the demands of the power ring.

In the forecourt was a fifty metre diameter scale relief globe of Garamas, slowly turning on its axis and showing the route of the great cable.

They stood in front of it for some minutes in silence. Even in model form, it was impressive.

Fletcher said, 'How come they let you in at all, if it's so restricted?'

'My father, Kaalba, is a Provincial Governor. He has travelled widely and he believes that women should have more opportunities. All the girls at the Polytech have influential contacts. But mostly they take language courses and social studies. They go into government departments as secretaries.'

'But that didn't appeal to you? You seem to have a fair arm lock on language yourself.'

'I have always had this interest in mathematics. My father trained as an engineer originally. There were instruction tapes in the library at home.'

'What does your mother think about it?'

'She is traditional. She accepts the conventions. But she could not go against my father's wishes. She does not like it.'

'She wouldn't like you to be mixed up with an underground group either.'

Yola said simply, 'No. But then you cannot avoid following your reason. That would be the greatest betrayal when you *understand* what must be done, you must try to do it. Many women who have stood up for human rights have been arrested and are in the internment camp here in Kristinobyl. We shall not rest until they are free.'

Back in his pad at the Space Terminal Hotel, Fletcher reckoned that she had a point. If he was left much longer on the beach, he would be taking a hand himself.

From the balcony, he could see more than half of the space port itself. On the perimeter, the two interned Scotian ships stood like minarets. In the foreground, freight and passenger ships from all points of the stellar compass were being serviced for take off. It was a sight that was a familiar part of his life and usually gave him uncomplicated pleasure with its blend of routine chores and high endeavour. Phoenician traders all, on their up-dated version of the wine-dark sea.

Usually he was involved in it. Preparing his own ship. This time, as a spectator, conditioned by knowledge of the hinterland, he was wide open to the winds of doubt. God, there was enough to do on every planet, without touting round the universe for more trouble. When his stint with I.G.O. was done, and that could be any day, if the enquiry pronounced against him, he ought to get back to Earth planet and cultivate his own garden. Keep a pig on the common and work at saying 'Arrh'.

Speculation cut off abruptly with a calling bleep from the video inside his room.

It was the I.G.O. commissar for Garamas in person, a squat Venusian, condemned to wear a ruff-like, air-adjustment unit to allow him to breathe the Garamasian atmosphere.

The gear was a sounding box for an already harsh voice and its metallic rasp was out of key with the surface courtesy of the text. Duvorac's large grey face filled the small screen and his eyes, golf-ball size with a hue of boiled spinach, seemed to have no part in it.

'Commander Fletcher, I hesitate to disturb you at this time; but I would be glad to see you in my office. There is a small matter in which you could help.'

'Now?'

'That would be most kind. I shall expect you in five minutes.'

'I'll be there.'

Seen close, Duvorac might have been an android torso, fused monolithically to a polished plinth. He was enclosed in a three sided executive console, which gave him a personalized information silo and minimized physical effort.

He wasted no time in getting down to basics. 'You will know, Commander, that the corvette *Petrel* is in the port. What you will not know is that there is nothing unserviceable about her. It was deliberate policy to keep her on that launch pad.'

Duvorac shifted a key with his left hand and a ground plan of Kristinobyl space port appeared on the blank wall behind him. He took a stylus to point to the miniature on his desk

17

top and an illuminated arrow tracked over the big screen.

'There she is, on the perimeter. It was the placing she was given, that determined our action. A lucky break, you might say. As you know, all military craft are allocated stations on the perimeter, at the maximum distance from the city and a defensive screen lies in an arc to seal them off from the rest of the port. That is standard practice. You will ask, why is the position of *Petrel* important?'

Dag Fletcher reckoned that for a man with a breathing problem the commissar was doing all right. To give him a break, he asked the question. 'Why is the position of *Petrel* important?'

Duvorac gave him a hard look as though filing it away for reference and went on, having a ready answer. 'From the ship it is possible to overlook the internment area. It is a large complex, where many thousands of persons are held. Mostly these are Garamasians, who have become unpopular with their government; but in one special sector there are some hundreds of foreign detainees . . .'

'As for instance, the crews of the two Scotian frigates?'

'Exactly. Also some of the crew of *Petrel*. They are not prisoners in an exact sense, you understand. But security is very strict. There are also many civilians, who for one reason or another do not have current visas. Often their stay is of short duration; until their own governments supply credentials. Amongst this group is an I.G.O. agent, who had information for us but was arrested on a minor infringement.'

'But I.G.O. will arrange release?'

'That is the difficulty. The agent is Fingalnan by birth. For I.G.O. to accept responsibility would be unusual. Fingalna has tended to be in the O.G.A. sphere of influence. At the moment, a routine enquiry has been made to Fingalna. The agent's cover was complex and will take some time to check.

18

But in the end, Fingalna is likely to repudiate citizenship. Under refined interrogation, the agent will talk.'

'This is very interesting, Commissar, but why do you tell me?'

Duvorac unexpectedly moved from his personal fortress and stamped out into the middle of his office. Height-wise, he could still have been sitting down. Hardly a metre and a half tall, he was like a mobile block of biological tissue, a compressed man; but impressive none the less.

Fletcher slewed round in his chair to stay facing the oracle and there was silence for a count of five.

Then Duvorac seemed to come to a decision, 'It is important that our agent is not questioned. Death would be preferable.'

Dag Fletcher stood up to say it. 'I am a spaceman not an assassin. Try somebody else.'

Duvorac was not impressed. 'You are quick, Commander; but in this case too quick. It may not come to that. I sincerely hope it will not. But you Earthmen continue to surprise me. You have a sentimental view of life. You would not hesitate to risk your own life or indeed to sacrifice a member of your crew in an engagament. A secret agent is also under orders. They are not children to be shielded from the harsh realities. However, to proceed. In the first instance, I want you to go aboard *Petrel*. Take a look at the layout of the internment area. I will give you a plan to assist orientation. Memorize the detail. Then return to me. I would rather outline my plan when you have a first-hand idea of the terrain. I trust you have no objection so far?'

'Getting aboard *Petrel* will be difficult. The military sector is sealed off.'

'A continuous power screen is expensive. It operates only a percentage of time. This is believed by the operators to be random. But we have observed it over a long period. We have matched the computer. Prediction is now reliable. I will give you the forecast for the next twenty four hours. That is more than enough.'

Duvorac returned to his pedestal and played himself another tune. A panel slid away and he fished out a small printed slip and a diagram. 'Memorize this sequence and destroy the paper. As you see, the next period is from fifteen hundred to fifteen thirty. It is now fourteen forty-one precisely. I suggest that you make a start right away. Here is the route which you are to take. You will find that it avoids all observation points. Once across the barrier, there is a system of blast trenches which will bring you below the gantry. All hatches were left on external manual.'

Action was welcome, but Fletcher reckoned that Duvorac was the optimist of all time to believe that a man could walk through a space port complex without a challenge. So far, he had been proved right; but the luck could hardly hold. Currently, he was threading a maze of metre-wide alleys, between slab-sided building blocks, walking in the bottom of a half-round culvert designed to carry away seasonal rain and now thick with white dust.

Ten metres ahead was the last intersection, brightly lit by direct sunlight shining along the gap, with a further twenty five metres of alleyway to the edge of the building zone. After that, it was open ground for fifty metres with the power field bisecting the area. If Duvorac's calculations were wrong, he would be crisped in a nonasecond.

The thought of it heightened sensitivity. He was a metre from the turn when the faint scuff of movement round the twist brought him to a halt.

Flat back against the wall, he peeled off his tunic, set his blaster for a wide-angle, stunning beam, shoved it in his waist-band and waited for the pay-off. Now he could hear the cat soft tread. It was someone familiar with the route, sure that he was safe. A Garamasian workman checking out the drainage.

An elongated shadow grew up the wall, supporting theory. But judgement took a knock, when an olive-drab uniformed leg preceded its owner into direct vision. Fletcher had a split second to recast his strategy with a sick, nervous dread in his stomach, which was the all-too familiar prelude to personal, physical action. He had planned to shroud the head to avoid recognition then lay the man cold for a two-hour stretch.

But the leg signalled that the wayfarer was a Scotian. Duvorac was not alone in his calculations. With or without Garamasian knowledge, the Scotian high Command was keeping a line open to their ships.

Reptile quick, the Scotian had sensed danger. He was round the corner in a twisty knot with a bulbous blaster sawing about for a target.

Fletcher grabbed for the wrist and the cold contact sent a galvanic surge through his body. Once in, he was okay. He had time to think that it might not always be so, that some time he might be inhibited by fear, whatever his mind wanted to do about it; then there was only the cold, efficient pattern of destruction.

Maybe the first shrinking of the nerves had a use in forcing a reaction. He felt his mind sharpened beyond normal, with every ongoing move crystal clear.

He took the Scotian's own kinetic urge and threw him into the culvert, then jumped down feet together as on to a landing pad.

Personal scores came into it. Knowledge of what The

Scotian had done to his own crewmen. When there was every reason to believe the man had a flat EEG, he still took his laser and drilled a pattern of bodkin holes in the narrow skull.

Nothing could look more dead than a dead Scotian. Ghoulish blue-white skin, reptile mouth gone slack showing the ridged bone that was the racial variant for teeth, pale eyes turned up to leave glaring pink disks. A gone scavenger.

They were the hatchet men of the O.G.A. organization, swarming from their dung-hued planet to pack into their deadly ships much as Northmen had packed the long boats that preyed on Europe in the long gone past. But without the Northman's heroic zest and barbaric splendour. They were cold, sadistic killers, without any code except expediency.

Fletcher knelt by the body and searched through the uniform pouches. There was nothing to give him a lead. That figured. They travelled light. Identity, stencilled on the left forearm claimed that he had been an executive in the power section of his ship, *Alope*—frigate class. Clan name Hathor. Number, birth group and dates of previous service. They carried the detail as a decoration.

Fletcher straightened up and checked the alley and the T-junction. Nothing moved. He went back and picked up the body, which was curiously lightweight for its size.

He went on at a quick walk, paused at the open end, then crossed the clear space at a jog trot. Only his subconscious was counting the metres and triggered off the signal to sweat at the half-way mark.

But Duvorac's timetable was holding up. In under fifty seconds, he was dropping into the first blast trench.

At the foot of *Petrel's* gantry, he stopped for a break. Leaving Hathor in the ditch, he hoisted himself up for a look round the set. From this point only the blank side of terminal buildings showed up like white cliffs. Nearer in, was a line of empty pads stretching in an arc either way with the two Scotian ships down left.

Using an elevator would show up as a power take on some engineer's console. He would have to climb. He lifted Hathor out and dumped him on the blast bed midway between *Petrel's* tripod jacks.

Here he was shielded, anyway, by the containing walls of the pit and inside the gantry, a sketchy run of cladding screened the ladders. But he could not help think that Duvorac had been over smooth. At any point, some security-minded official at Mission Control might run a scan to see that all was well with the idle ships.

At the main hatch, there was no cover. He crossed a ten-metre gangway on his belly and only stood up against the I.G.O. blazon, where he reckoned the pattern would be camouflage enough.

Inside, he felt more at home than anytime in the last ten days. *Petrel* was a more recent *marque* than *Terrapin*; but the layout was not much different. He went through the lock into a small reception area and through again into the narrow central trunk that communicated with all modules.

First he dropped down under gravity, through the power pack to the freight bay which doubled as ship's hospital. There, be broke out a disposal sack and lowered a hook to pick up the Scotian.

Within two hours there would be nothing for anybody to find of Hathor.

Then he activated the moving grab line and hauled himself two hundred metres into the cone.

As Duvorac had predicted, the view from the forward gunnery module might have been set up for visual recce of the internment complex. Using the powerful direct vision scopes, he quartered the area.

Fifteen minutes close work and Fletcher was confident he could walk round the cage without a guide. He still had an hour before the next break in the power screen. He dropped to the command cabin and sat on the gymbol mounted acceleration couch on the command island. Circling slowly, he remembered *Terrapin* as she made the last course change that strained every centimetre of her hull and sent her streaking in for the kill.

A tell-tale on the communication's desk bleeped for a half minute before he recognized that it was not sounding in his mind.

It was one way traffic and scrambled at that. But a tape punched it out in clear for him to read off. 'Screen on full operation. Stay.'

It was just as well he had visited the control cabin. Duvorac's master-mind was too fond of long shots for comfort. But then, like the man said, individuals were expendable in the public interest. You just had to take a professional view.

CHAPTER TWO

DAG Fletcher fixed himself a meal at the ward room dispenser and ate with one ear cocked for a summoning bleep on the communications console.

Two hours moving round the ship proved Duvorac dead right on one score. She was all systems go. Except for the gantry, locked on at two points, she was ready to blast off.

Outside light levels began to drop. Twilight on Garamas was uniform and fast. Light a cigarette in broad day and you could flick its glowing stub in an arc against black night. But before dusk made true darkness, there was a recrudescence of cinnamon light, a curious warm glow that was a unique feature of the planet.

Fletcher stood by a direct vision port waiting for it, looking over towards Kristinobyl—a filigree of light. From this angle, it could be anywhere he had ever been. European Space Corporation complex looked like that from ships on the perimeter. All cats grey in the dark. Where did that get him, anyway?

It was more a time for nostalgia than for deep thought. A time of diffused excitement with no focus. A feeling that anything was possible; that anything might develop from this minute now, which would change the future. Nothing ever did. But he recognized that it was important to believe that it could. Without some expectation that the future could be changed, that a man's past and present were not necessarily a strait-jacket on him, there would be no reason to go on.

Brought up by a cosmic dimmer, the set flooded briefly with reddish-brown. Kristinobyl put on a structured skin and appeared solidly on the cyclorama. Every detail was momentarily clear, before a smooth fade out into deep blackness that picked out the sky as a star map.

Fletcher moved as the light went to look across at the Scotian frigates. He was left with a picture on his retina, that persisted against the black curtain. Below the freight hatch on the nearer ship, there had been a blurred movement. His mind tried to fill out the pattern from the clues and supplied a full-colour version of a green-uniformed Scotian being winched smartly aboard by a hoist line.

Reason could find no flaw. In two minutes, he was convinced that it was what he had seen. Well, that figured. Hathor had been returning from his ship. They probably had a watch detail working. Regular changes. Keep all hands on a war footing.

Fletcher moved restlessly about the silent ship. Knowledge that Scotians were aboard their craft was unsettling. It turned the two silent landmarks into strongpoints. For a sure thing, units of the main armament would be trained on *Petrel* as a starting gambit.

Habit died hard. She was not his ship; but as the only executive on the site, he was responsible for her safety. He climbed again to the gunnery module, picked up the Scotians on a direction grid and lined up a destructor beam for each mid-ship's module.

Hair trigger relays were set to fall on detection of enemy fire. If *Petrel* was hit, a split second later, the Scotians would join her as molecular scrap.

It was a certain fragment to shore against time's ruin; but not enough. Fletcher took another look at the communications desk. No dice. Duvorac was temporarily out of programme.

He gave him ten minutes and spent the time sorting through the communications locker for monitor gear. A compressed air pistol, with a clip of pea-sized adhesive transmitter buttons was the handiest choice. Range marked on the butt was two hundred metres; but he reckoned he would have to get nearer than that to hit even a frigate in the dark.

He shoved it in his belt to leave his hands free and let himself out by the main hatch.

Up aloft, there had seemed to be enough light to work by, with the nimbus thrown up by Kristinobyl and the stars, but at ground level, he was shadowed by solid structures. He allowed himself a miserly beam from a hooded torch to get clear of the gantry and dropped into a blast trench that ran towards the Scotians.

After three intersections, on a dog-leg course, he calculated that he was over half way and coming up to extreme range for the pistol. The rim of the trench was at finger-tip stretch and he went up in a silent heave.

Lying flat, he closed his eyes and opened them slowly. The frigates were dead ahead, a thickening of darkness on darkness. He went along on hands and knees feeling a way forward for the next intersection.

He hit it twenty metres on and the targets were clearer. Now it was possible to separate the slim cylinder of the nearer ship from its gantry. But not near enough to be sure. He dropped into the trench, and went up the other side.

This time, there was a long run, on the lip of a primary channel that fanned out from the pad and took the first surge of flame from the rocket motors.

Fifty metres from the tripod jacks, he knelt like a marksman with the pistol steadied by knee and arm and fired three times, spacing them out from the freight module to the cone.

27

Reaching the far ship took longer. There was more on the ground than he had seen from *Petrel;* storage crates, parked surface craft and a fuelling tender. When he checked his time disk, he found he had been two hours on the mission. He planted four, five and six and turned back.

Moving towards light was easier and he made better time. *Petrel*'s gantry was only twenty metres off, when the nudge of a sixth sense pulled him up short.

Back to the stone wall of his gully, he tried to sort out impressions. *Petrel* and the girder work of the gantry, were fused in a continuous blur. Imagination played tricks. There could be movement anywhere at all. He told himself he was being over-cautious and began to move forward. Then a tiny metallic click orientated him. Whatever was there, was at ground level.

Suddenly he knew how it would be. Two could play the eavesdropping game. It would have to be a party from the first ship, otherwise he would have met them head on. While he was circling farther out to get at the second rocket, they had gotten ahead. Then he must have followed along.

Instinct had him debating how to cut them down. But the ongoing implication of that held him back. Successful or not, it would put a finger on *Petrel* for sure. So far, they would have no clue of what had happened to Hathor. He might have disappeared in Kristinobyl. They were just leaving no stone unturned. He could see the cold mind of a Scotian commander handling the problem and checking every angle, however improbable.

As of now, there was nothing to pick up from the Earth ship. They should be allowed to report back with a negative. All he needed to know was what kind of device they had fixed.

He got himself out of the channel, feeling the weight of his body. It was getting to be a hard night. At the top, he slipped out of his shoes, shoved one in either pocket of his tunic, and moved along making no sound, until he was fending off from the gantry cladding with the finger tips of both hands.

His ears picked up on a-tonal dry clicking, very quiet, like a muted and slowed-down cicada.

There was some satisfaction in having a theory confirmed. Not that he could understand it. Scotian speech was one on its own, a grouping of palatal clicks in a code that only a semantics computer could crack.

They were over left by a gap in the structure through which he had left. Walking in through there, would have set him up as a target against the dim light.

Patiently, moving a centimetre at a time, Fletcher felt his way along the cladding to the next open section. He was working round the freight elevator trunk and they were very close. More clicks, which carried a sense of finality. They were through. He heard the pad of feet moving away and swivelled round his corner.

Between the lattice of the cage, he picked out two shadowy forms going home.

It took all of fifteen minutes to find the box and when he had it, he was not sure that it was a recent plant or part of the existing circuits of the gantry. Fixed knee-high in the angle of a girder, it would be lost even in broad day. A fine multi-core cable plugged into the case and ran aloft, neatly strapped every metre.

Confirmation came, when he traced the lead through and found a saucer-shaped suction cup at the business end like a blister on the underside of the freight bay.

They had gone in for substantial gear; a single unit, but powerful enough to pick up sound from anywhere in the ship. Also, with a remote-sited transmitter, it would not show, if the ship ran a check for a bug fixed to its outer skin.

He went back and disconnected the transmitter, then made his way through the main hatch.

Nothing had changed. He fixed himself some coffee and took it into the command module. Working with a hooded light on the communications desk, he clipped the gun to an amplifier circuit, that would deliver its catch through the tannoy and filter speech through the language cracker.

One at a time, he brought in the six transmitter buttons. One and two on the first ship were dead. Three brought in breathing and a slow heart beat. That figured. They were using the cone module as a watch tower. One man there. Two out on the mission. Duty detail of three. Maybe one changed each day. He had been lucky. Hathor's relief man might have been right behind him.

Four, five and six were dead. So the second ship had no permanent crew. Back with number one button, he waited for the two men to come home. There was time to consider the strangeness of what he was doing, alone in the silent corvette. Earth was infinitely distant. He was a speck, an itinerant consciousness with no point of reference, performing bizarre actions for no reason. I think therefore I am. Or, I act therefore I am? Speculation cut off, as the whine of a winch sounded out startlingly close. A cable ran out and retracted. Brief speech, followed by the chatter of his own computer, as it punched out a translation.

He read it off as he tracked them through the ship.

'Report to Urion. I will switch the receiver to module one.'
'Check.'

Button two picked up the action in the command module. Button three brought in Urion, the executive in charge.

'Well?'

'It is done lieutenant. Norops is switching through. There was no sign that the Earth ship is manned.'

'No sign of Hathor?'

'No, lieutenant.'

'He said nothing to you before he left?'

'No, lieutenant.'

'Nevertheless, you will be interrogated.'

Fletcher found it hard to sympathize with a Scotian, but he recognized it was rough on the man. Interrogation in that service could mean anything up to piecemeal dismemberment. In this case, with trained space crew thin on the ground, they would probably stop short of anything that would damage his efficiency. But it would be bad. It was an everlasting surprise that the rank-and-file never mutinied. As far as it was known, there was no case on record of a Scotian crew shedding a Captain Bligh and setting up on an atoll.

The printed dialogue remained cool. Discipline was built in from an early age.

'I know nothing, lieutenant.'

'We shall see.'

A second delivery slot on the communications desk put out another tape. It was Duvorac, getting in on the act with an all-clear. 'Screen reverted. Use next period. Report 1100.'

There was under seven minutes. Fletcher cleared away all traces of his visit with brisk economical movements. I act therefore I am. Maybe that was the truth for him. Purposeful occupation conferred identity, he was better following orders.

On the way out, he reconnected the Scotian transmitter. Let them drink their fill of silence. One thing was a stone hard certainty, there would be a round-the-clock vigil at the other end for as long as *Petrel* remained on her pad.

Kristinobyl was perking up for the night shift. The business quarter was blacked out, but the pleasure domes of the entertainment sector were taking a double ration of power from the grid. In the lobby of the Space Terminal Hotel, Fletcher debated whether or not to take an auto-shuttle and go out for a drink. But the isolation of the last hours had cut back appetite for the social scene. Instead, he stopped off at the tenth floor Vista Bar and carried his glass out on the balcony.

Revellers were thin on the ground and he had it to himself. He leaned on the rail, looking out down a broad avenue, with illuminated fountains, towards the city centre where the action was. There was enough muted noise flowing in, to mask any sound at his back and the thin querulous voice, speaking in English that sounded a metre behind his left ear seemed to have arrived by spontaneous creation.

There was no doubt about the solidity of its owner, however. He had gained a full-sized Garamasian, all in black, with a high-crowned peaked cap, carrying the three intertwined rings of the security service.

'Commander Fletcher?'

'The same.'

'You are not easy to find. I have made two visits here today. No one was able to tell me where you had gone.'

If the statement concealed a question it was doomed to frustration. Fletcher said, 'Well, now you have me. What did you want to see me about?'

'I am Colonel Pedasun, Government Security Service.'

It was his bad night for reactions. If he expected his hearer to drop his glass and clutch the balcony with both hands, he had another disappointment.

'You have done well.'

Pedasun's black eye disks were unruffled by any catspaw of emotion, but he had recognized the answer as frivolous.

'I understand that Earthmen are not serious minded. But you will find that the position of a foreigner in Garamas is

32

not some joke. I have come myself so that you will appreciate the gravity of the situation you are in.'

'What situation?'

'In the first place you have made a bad choice of assistant. The girl Yola is unreliable. There is suspicion at least that she is involved with an extremist student group which will soon be on the proscribed list. She has been tolerated so far out of respect for her father, who is an important man.'

'She is a very efficient interpreter. As far as I know, she is also a very conscientious student. I would not see her as a danger to the state.'

'But then as an Earthman you would not know about the peculiar delicacy of our political scene. You have visited the Science Wing at the Polytech. Why was that?'

'To see how the other half live.'

'Where have you been today?'

'Around and about in Kristinobyl. No special place.'

'A long period for random sightseeing.'

'Places interest me.'

'I will be frank with you and expect frankness in return. As you will know, there are two Scotian frigates impounded in the port. Part of the crews are on open survelliance in the town. They have been here a long time and close captivity would be unreasonable. One of the men has disappeared. It is known that Earth and Scotia are bitterly opposed. It could be that you met this man and were provoked into combat. If that is so and you can throw light on the affair, you should tell me now. It may be possible to hush it up. The Scotian command naturally are pressing for a full investigation.'

'I can't help you.'

'Can not or will not? I can assure you, if you are involved and this comes out in an open enquiry, your organization will be powerless to assist you.'

'Why out of the millions in Kristinobyl do you come to me? It doesn't make any sense.'

Pedasun walked to the rail and looked out over the city. Fletcher finished his drink and stood the glass on a handy table. His last question hung about unanswered. A group of Garamasians in animated discussion, like the overflow from a convention, came through to the balcony, saw the black uniform and went out in sudden silence.

It reminded Fletcher that he was pushing his luck. Duvorac might well be poking grapes through the bars at him by the time of tomorrow's tryst.

On the other hand, there was no good way of handling a type like Pedasun. Take a conciliatory line and he would tramp all over the psyche. He soldiered on as if he had not noticed the hiatus in the dialogue. 'Nice to have met you, Colonel. Sorry I can't help you with your problem. Check the zoo. Your missing man might have strayed into a reptile house and found it to his liking. See you again, no doubt.'

He was five metres off before Pedasun realised he was losing his audience. Garamasian facial geography was a natural for a mine of malice and Fletcher was lucky not to see it. The voice carried a harmonic of it, however, as the security man spoke over his shoulder. 'I am quite sure, we shall meet again, Commander. Do not leave Kristinobyl without notifying my office.'

Duvorac looked as though he had not moved in the intervening hours. Given the Venusian's ability to operate for several days without sleep, that could have been true. His first question was hardly more friendly in tone than Pedasun's and Dag Fletcher had a case in wondering whose side he was on.

34

'Why did you find it necessary to kill the Scotian? It has caused serious diplomatic difficulty at a time when we do not want embarrassment.'

Fletcher reckoned he had been at the receiving end long enough. He had taken a seat opposite the human cuboid. It enabled him to stand up as though walking out. 'I take it there would have been equal embarrassment in having to explain why I was found dead on the route to the military zone. If you do not trust me to use my discretion in any situation you should find someone else for your operation.'

Duvorac switched to conciliation and even tried to smile, knowing from a theoretical point of view that it was a sign of fair intent in the Earth culture.

The net product was an amalgam of the sinister and the malevolent; but clued in by the voice, it lost some of its visual shock. He said mildly, 'Pray sit down again, Commander. You are too hasty. I have the highest regard for your abilities. Tell me how you found the ship.'

Fletcher took his time to get back to his seat, making it clear that he was still in doubt about going on. Military assessment was a neutral field however and an I.G.O. Commissar had every right to his opinion. 'She's sound. Ready to go. I had time to check her through. A very efficient unit.'

'And the Scotians?'

'I was coming to that. One with a watch detail. One not. I fixed pickups on both. They have no idea what happened to their man.'

'That was very enterprising of you.'

The tone was ambivalent. Fletcher took a sharp look at the Commissar to try to judge whether that was a straight comment. He might as well have searched for a ripple on an egg. He soldiered on with the plain tale. 'They had the same idea. *Petrel* is hooked up on a monitor.'

Some animation crept into Duvorac's tone. 'That is bad. They will know that you were there.'

'Not so. As far as that goes they believe she is empty. We can diss their gear any time for a period.'

'Very good. You have a flair for this work, Commander.'

Fletcher waited for it. Flattery was ever a prelude for a dicey proposition. He was not wrong. Duvorac went on, 'How would Yola react to an opportunity for helping some of the members of her group who are interned at the detention centre?'

It was pointless to ask what the man knew about Yola's extra-curricular activities. Obviously, there was very little on Garamas that escaped his net.

'She would take it. But she shouldn't be asked. Security already have her number. I had a visit from a certain Colonel Pedasun who left me in no doubt.'

'Pedasun is shrewd but limited. What I have in mind is a demonstration outside the centre, which would cause a certain amount of confusion. It would be timed to coincide with a visit you would make to the crew of *Petrel*. Our agent would take the chance to hide in your car. You would leave while the guards were still concerned in looking outwards for a threat.'

'Very psychological. Suppose they search?'

'That would be unfortunate. But the agent would not betray you. It would be an opportunist move. You would not be implicated.'

In spite of ceremonial rig and a plushy official car with the I.G.O. pennant streaming from the transom, Fletcher graded himself as the rat of all time, when he answered a smart salute and idled through the check point at the internment camp.

Yola had been easy. Taken it as progress, to get a visitor

36

interested in the cause. She had sold it to the group and it had spread to all who looked on the internment camp as a symbol of unpopular government and every faction could identify somewhere. They had worked day and night on a plan for Kristinobyl's first essay in student demo. Small groups had been leaving the city for hours. They were to dress in white—the traditional colour of mourning—and assemble at the main gate, then walk in silence round the compound. Not revolution, red in tooth and claw; but a big step for people sold on the obedience ticket from the crib.

Fletcher had passed some of them on the road. Very excited and talkative, very naïve. He felt old in guile, a corrupter of youth.

His driver presented the I.G.O. pass. A guard walked the length of the shuttle, looking in through the plexiglass dome and waving them on with another snappy salute.

Inside, they crossed an open courtyard and sidled in under a canopy for Fletcher to make a status building entrance to the reception area. He let anyone who was interested, hear him say. 'I'll be thirty minutes. Be here at fifteen-forty-five.'

The car pulled away to wait in a parking lot behind the main building and he went on into the lobby.

Gilded cage notwithstanding, *Petrel*'s skeleton crew, when he found them, were ripe for mayhem. Even Cotgrave, a phlegmatic, square-built man, with a round, open face, co-pilot and acting Commander of the unit, was at the far edge of tolerance.

He said, 'Look, Commander, you can tell Varley we've had enough. What in hell is he playing at? Why can't *Petrel* rejoin the fleet? She was on an official visit with the squadron. There was no call for internment. I reckon if somebody got their finger out, she could be operational tomorrow. We've had enough of these goons and that's a fact.'

Six others crowded round to get the news from home and there was no disguising the fact that they resented the I.G.O. rep.

Fletcher found it an unusual experience and one he could have done without. Here were seven highly trained space men rotting on the beach and he had been angled into the slot of a visiting staff type handing out the establishment line.

Cotgrave remembered protocol with an obvious effort and introduced him round. There were two from each section. Enough to make *Petrel* a viable proposition for a short haul. Bennett and Sluman from Navigation; Johnson and Ledsham from Communications; Engles and Hocker from Power.

On free choice, he wouldn't have taken any one in a crew. They were sour and argumentative. Morale had taken a knock or rather had been slowly drained off. If there had been any real hardship it would have been better for discipline.

Fletcher told himself to suspend judgement and tried to make contact. After ten minutes, he recognized that he was making out, except with Dave Hocker, youngest of the group, a large-boned, dark-haired type who carried a mammoth chip about chair-borne administrators who, on his analysis, wouldn't know a rocket ship from their own ass.

If there had been no background complication, Dag Fletcher would have been nettled by it. As it was, there was an exercise in managerial techniques to keep his mind off sin. He handed out a batch of mail and some of the tension went out. He took Cotgrave aside.

'What's with this Hocker?'

'Don't take too much notice of the boys just now. They've had a bellyful. It was a bad mission, before ever we got here. Hocker's a good man at his job. I'll agree he knows it. He was disappointed when Engels was made executive. We lost Power One with the captain.'

Fletcher looked at the time disk. Bang on the nose. God, it was asking a lot from a mob of amateurs to hit a precise time on a big operation. Duvorac was the optimist of the century.

Bennett a small wiry figure with a narrow, intelligent face and a shock of very black hair, called over from the window that filled one side of the common room, 'Skipper. Look out here. Something's worrying the goons. They're all over the place.'

Garamasian guards were appearing at the double to form up on the square. Late comers were still buttoning tunics. The keening wail of a siren started up as Cotgrave moved.

Lining the window, the Earthmen watched an officer, using a powered megaphone, walk down the line. Garamasian gobbledegook filtered through the double glazing.

Cotgrave said, 'Maybe it's a break out. What do you say, Commander?'

The crackle of a tannoy from a roof grille answered for him. A Garamasian voice using stilted English said, 'All detainees are instructed to return to their quarters. Do not leave your sleeping space. Anyone moving in the open will be shot on sight. All visitors must leave now.'

Sticks of soldiery were peeling off. Files of eight—the Garamasian basic number. Running jerkily to emergency stations on the perimeter. Except that they were not waving riot sticks and nobody fell flat in a mud patch, it was like watching a historic, silent movie.

Cotgrave said, 'You'd better get clear, Commander. Do no good to get you interned for ignoring that order. They're dead touchy about regs. Half the residents hardly know why they're inside. We'll see you again?'

'I'll work on it. *Petrel* may be cleared for service any time. Be ready for that.'

He tried to pack a significant look into it, remembering that rooms in this complex would be monitored and Cotgrave nodded.

'We'll be ready. As of now, we'll do like the man said and go back to the cells.'

In reception, there were others waiting for transport out. Three Garamasians, who looked like legal consultants and a Scotian with the sleeve braid of a lieutenant, who stood apart and tracked Fletcher through with a cold glare.

He walked straight to the desk and asked for his car to be called. Without looking up, the Garamasian orderly spoke rapidly into an intercom. A small thing, but a kind of insolence and Fletcher realized that the rank and file had no time for I.G.O.

Using speech tones, he said, 'What is the emergency about?'

The man went on checking a list.

Fletcher leaned over took the slack of his tunic at the neck, and gave a shake, 'What is the emergency about?'

This time he got attention. The man used English and fairly spat out, 'Some young fools are assembled at the gate. Your ideas of civil disturbance have caught on. You will see how we deal with it.'

That was a point. Yola and her friends could be in more danger than they knew. Too many for mass arrest, but some punitive action would follow for sure.

The I.G.O. car edged in to the bay. He marched across to it and got in. There was nothing to see and he thought that Duvorac had been too optimistic. In some ways it was a relief. The demonstration was not being cynically used for another purpose. They would have to try again, with a military-type, cutting out operation.

At the check point, the same guard saw them through. Duvorac had guessed right on that count. There was no detailed search. Even as he walked the length of the car, the man kept looking over his shoulder at the uncharacteristic action going on outside.

A fifty-metre clear area surrounded the complex. Drawn up midway in the space, on a hundred-metre front, was a solid eight-deep phalanx of silent, white figures holding a wake.

The organizers had done well. It was an impressive sight. The silence of so many was a tangible thing.

Fletcher's car turned out of the barrier and moved slowly between the camp wall and the leading file. He tried to pick out Yola, but she could have been any one of a dozen, anonymous shrouded figures.

As they cleared the end marker, and rose ten metres to their flight lane, a tannoy spoke from a watch tower set on high stilts over the flat roof of the gatehouse.

Fletcher said, 'Slow,' and slewed round in his seat.

There was no movement from the silent ranks. A file of guards lined the parapet.

The car was nearing an intersection, where they would pick the ring road for Kristinobyl. Suddenly Fletcher knew how it would be. Following honourable precedent, the Commandant would try a whiff of grapeshot.

His order to 'Turn around. Run between the crowd and the gate,' was still echoing round the shuttle, when pinpoints of red flame blossomed briefly all along the firestep.

A long swathe of the front rank were down, some to stay, some crawling random fashion to get clear. Both ends of the column broke and ran for it. From above, the white line seemed to have been stretched suddenly like elastic and snapped at its centre.

The guards fired again methodically picking off the stragglers.

Fletcher said again, gritty with anger that swamped out every other factor, 'Back. Turn around and go back.'

There was no answer. When he whipped round, ready to pluck the man from his console and take it himself, he had to concede that the man had his problems.

A silvery Fingalnan girl had wriggled from under the squab like an adder, looking infinitely delicate and fragile in a taut, lime-green leotard, which could have been sprayed on by a niggardly make-up artist.

Feminine charm could only go so far. Currently, she was sticking a slender stiletto a millimetre or so into the side of the engineer's neck and her voice was full of conviction. Bell-like in timbre, it had a bizarre way with English.

'Not so Commandaire. I am sorree to seem obstetrical, but we 'ave to be real queek. Som omelette ees not made without breaking som egg. Do not worree. Much good will com. Make people theenk, I guesss. We drive on. I am Xenia.'

Behind them, the one-way battle was over. All who could had gone. The guards had stopped firing. Only a medical tender would be welcome.

Fletcher was coldly angry. He saw that Duvorac had only told half a tale. He must have known what was likely to happen. He had also known that the agent was a girl. It was time he took a personal line or they would walk all over him.

He leaned forward casually as though accepting the situation. Then his hands shot over the squab and plucked her out of her bucket seat.

For a count of five, it was as if he had hauled a small hot shark aboard a dinghy. He was reminded that Fingalnian metabolism kept its daughters' blood a good five degrees higher than his own. He was grappling with a tricky, polystyrene model. Then he damped down all action by sheer body weight.

He called over to his driver who was still bemused and rubbing his neck, 'Call Kristinobyl General Hospital. Say it's a multiple accident. Make it urgent. Then get back to I.G.O.'

To his pneumatic bedfellow, now trying to sink a neat set of white teeth into his shoulder, he said, 'Relax. Tell me all about yourself.'

CHAPTER THREE

DUVORAC had Xenia at his right hand, an incongruous running mate. She was perched lightly on a high stool, only lacking a chromium bar rail to fill out the set. A faint sandalwood perfume drifted out as from a smouldering joss stick. Wide-open, green eyes, dramatized by clever shading and an oblique flare of eyebrow, never left Fletcher's face.

He got the feeling that, in a general way, she was reading his mind, before he had actually sorted his ideas into a form of words. That figured. As he recalled, E.S.P. was a finely-developed art on her home planet. He made a note that on any important issue, he would have to keep information from the transfer areas of his brain and consciously use masking techniques.

As of now it was robbing what he had to say of some impact. He could have signed off and let the two of them get on with it. But he could still see the quiet patient ranks of young Garamasians being chopped down. Somebody had to be ombudsman.

He wound up with, 'I know all the argument about ends and means. I'll concede that *vis-a-vis* O.G.A. we can't afford to lose. But I don't go along with massacres of the innocent. Count me right out.'

Xenia's green eyes remained unblinking and unfathomable. He could tell that she was trying to probe behind the manifest for fissures of insincerity. Taking advantage of her concentration, he cleared his mind and tried to use its still centre as a crystal, ready to vibrate to any signal she might be sending on her own account.

There was nothing precise to register. Only a conviction that she was completely amoral. Right and wrong were interesting abstractions that made other people tick, but carried no imperatives. She would judge every situation on its merits for its balance of advantage.

Even at that, she must be loyal or a wily operator like Duvorac would have no use for her. Also, selection for the I.G.O. service was thorough and tough.

Xenia gave open proof that she was digging around in his head. 'You worree about me, Commandaire. That eees naice, I guess. We weell get on veray well togethaire.'

'You haven't been listening. I've done my stint as a fifth column.'

Duvorac judged that the junior ranks had talked enough. He fished about on his console and found a printed signal. Speaking as he handed it out, he said, 'I must remind you, Commander, that in war, there are things to be done which no one likes. None of us has any choice. Neither me nor you.'

The directive was brief enough and was signed by Varley. Key sentence read, 'Until the findings of the enquiry into the loss of *Terrapin* are published Commander D. Fletcher is seconded for service with the I.G.O. Consulate on Garamas. He will accept instructions given personally by the I.G.O. Commissar for Garamas under the terms of military service requirements.'

So there it was in print alive, so he could be sure it was true. Unless Duvorac had cooked it up to strengthen his arm.

The thought had barely formed when Xenia said, 'I was

45

here when eet came through, Commandaire. There ees no deception.'

Fletcher said, 'An oath is an oath. I accept that. Also a man is a man. You will have to accept that. If you go beyond what I believe is right, I shall say so.'

'You are able to judge that better than I can? I have noticed before that Earthmen have a built-in arrogance, which is often unsupported by real understanding. However, Commander, I think you will begin to appreciate the problems we face, when I tell you what Xenia here has been doing.'

Xenia, moved by some unexpected residue of modesty, left her high seat and walked behind Fletcher's chair leaving a pollen cloud that would set her up as a prime mover in Garamasian café society.

Duvorac went on, 'She has penetrated a number of organizations in Kristinobyl and neighbouring cities. There is no doubt at all that preparations are well under way to force a *coup d'état* and put in power an extreme right-wing government, which would take the planet into the O.G.A. sphere. Indeed O.G.A. agents are active in these groups, Scotians, Sabazians, and Laodamians. They seem confident that there will be no opposition—though you know yourself that many of the young people have radical views.'

There was a pause. Xenia had wandered near the back of his chair and Fletcher could feel convection currents as if from a free standing heater. It needed a direct question to get his mind on the agenda and Duvorac supplied it. 'What do you know of the Laodamians, Commander?'

'Not much. They're well inside O.G.A. space. I.G.O. military ships never visit. I was there, for a brief stopover, in a European Space Corporation freighter. Never left the space port. Hominoid. Advanced. Look like gorillas, but that's deceptive. Technically very smart. Taken public persuasion techniques as far as they go. Beyond what is permitted under the I.G.O. Charter of Human Rights. I recall now, we had the ship under full screening all the time we were in the gravisphere.'

'Thank you, Commander. Very useful. That is so, of course. Why would there be Laodamians in these underground groups?'

'If a *putsch* is intended, they could be useful to soften up public opinion.'

'That is what I think. But you can see it is important that we *know* what methods are to be used. Then we can develop a counterstrike.'

'What about the government? They ought to do something about it.'

'The official government is undermined by traitors. It is unable to do anything against this strong minority, which has allies amongst all the old ruling families. No, we have to save them from themselves without being seen to do so.'

'I see that. What do you want me to do?'

'Work with Xenia. There is one investigation you can make right away. She has identified a regular meeting place outside Kristinobyl. There is a growing cache of technical equipment. You may be able to decide how it is to be used.'

'An engineer would be a better choice.'

'You are too modest, Commander. I have been studying your service profile. It is very impressive.'

Xenia said, 'I like eet, also.'

The people's choice stood up 'When do we start?'

'Very soon. First the back room boys will fix you a new identity. Also a new face. Don't be alarmed No surgery. Just a thin plastic skin that goes on and comes off like a mask. Good luck.'

47

Standing in Kristinobyl's main square, waiting for Xenia to meet him under the clock, Fletcher felt integrated with the heavy-class intriguers of all time. The make-up syndicate had done a good job. His face had been given a square-ish cast. Looking at himself after the event, he had believed it was a trick mirror. He couldn't recognize himself which ought to be good enough.

Ethnic stock was more difficult to hide, so he was a civilian Earthman, one of the many who lived and worked in the cosmopolitan business sector of Kristinobyl. Papers identified him as Harry Fenton, a technical assistant in a firm of micro switchgear importers.

When she arrived with a quick, buoyant step, Xenia could have been any small, dark Eastern-European type keeping a date. Straight back hair swung silkily to her shoulders; skilful colouring masked normal skin pallor; a loving artist in foam plastic had given her ogee arch treatment under her tabard to rival an Apsaras.

Only the hand she put on his arm was out of character. Its warmth was electric. She said, ambiguously, 'How do you laike eet, Harree?'

It was a big question, so he played for time with 'I can take it or leave it.' Her throaty giggle earned a blank stare from a traditional Garamasian matron in a black caftan, who was walking the statutory half pace behind her husband. They were in business as a vaudeville team.

After the initial strangeness, Fletcher recognized that he was enjoying the experience. He had always been aware of his own tendency to act out a part and stand aside as a spectator while it was going on, almost in self-mockery. But there had always been an undertone of unresolved guilt, as though he knew he should not be doing it. He had always envied men like Cameron of *Hawk*, who were totally outgoing and never had a

48

doubt about their mission. This was a holiday for a schizo. Split personality in the line of duty. He began to elaborate on the role.

Working round to the downtown area, where a car for a run outside the city could be hired without question, he took his lush Semite into an actualities arena. On the huge oval stage the 3-D projections were working diligently through a complicated orgy sequence that would have had De Sade clapping his hands with childlike glee.

Fletcher said, 'Do you notice anything?'

'What am I supposed to look at, Harree? Ees eet som special trick you laike me to remembaire in case we make love? Thees ees a naice new side to your nature. I thought you Earthmen were prunes.'

'Not on the stage. Round about.'

'Menee Scotians.'

'That's so. This would draw them in. Like setting a jam pot for wasps.'

Three metres off a Scotian turned slowly in his seat and stared at Xenia; a satanshape for any Walpurgis night. His face was a set mask with a dribble of thin liquid from the corners of the mouth. He had obviously suspended disbelief and was getting his catharsis in the best tradition of dramatic art, but something had disturbed concentration.

Fletcher put his arm casually round the girl and walked her away towards a refreshment buffet.

He said, 'There's a thing. They can give you a new contour, but they can't alter your metabolism. That one had picked up your high-grade, thermal agitation. You should be kept strictly on ice. We must remember that. Scotians have long range radar for little, hot-blooded females.'

'But not Earthmen, Harree? How do you get to be so cold and calculating?'

'It's just a knack.'

'Knack? What ees thees "knack"?'

'Never mind. Maybe I'll let you see it sometime.'

'Don't trifle with a defenceless girl, Harree.'

It was all good knockabout stuff, but Fletcher reckoned they ought to get on before she reached out for a custard pie.

They circulated slowly for the far exit and picked up a shuttle from the rank. Xenia did some quick dialling on the auto setter and they sat in the rumble under an observation dome.

Every architectural style in the Galaxy had been tried out in Kristinobyl. Out of the centre, which was being redeveloped as tower cores with plug-in capsules on a basic lattice, there was a time gap in every suburb. Heavy *mastabas* in the traditional Garamasian style, blank to the street, with a maze of alleys in the rear; slender Fingalnan accommodation units like minarets; even a quarter of bizarre, black and white cottages with twisted chimney stacks. They had tried to be all things to all men.

Outside city limits, they crossed a belt of mauve *erichthonius,* spread out below like an embroidered cloth. They were in the flight lane for the nearest city to the capital, the manufacturing centre Bunomion, twenty kilometres distant and concealed by a low range of hills.

Conscious that any general duty car would be monitored Fletcher said, 'What's at Bumonion, then? Do we want to spend our golden hours looking at Garamasian-style industry?'

'There ees som leetle park over the hill. Veray prettee. We can walk about and you can hold my hand.'

As if on cue, the car rose ten metres to clear a spur and planed down into a parking lot, with a long streamer banner bearing a legend in gobbledegook Garamasian, which was already two-thirds full of private, family shuttles. Close by the terminal, there was an entertainment area and a milling crowd of Garamasian children moved jerkily through sequences leading to the illusion of having a carefree time. Outside the air-conditioned car, they were struck by a wave of heat as though opening the door of a furnace.

Xenia said, 'The car will wait two hours for us. So we must watch the time. Otherwise eet ees som long walk back, I guess.'

She led off at a brisk walk for the open heath.

Narrow paths crisscrossed the reserve. From the flank of the hill, they could look down to a natural lake, maybe a kilometre long and half that broad. The mauve *erichthonius* plant, which was the standard growth on every open space on Garamas ran down to the water's edge. More mature citizens were finding simple pleasures under the sun, dotted here and there on the grass in entwined units of two. In this enclave, sexual inequality was in abeyance.

In the centre of the lake was a small, irregular-shaped island, heavily wooded with pale yellow cycads. Electric power boats were weaving about in silence, as though drawn by under-water cables.

In fact, silence was the dominating feature on the set. Remembering Coney Island play areas on Earth planet, Fletcher told himself that the Garamasian ethnic type was way ahead on some counts. Close your eyes and you could imagine you were alone. Which was how many, no doubt, were playing their tape.

He checked it out and stumbled over a small rock.

Xenia said, 'What ees eet, Harree? Does eet worree you to be alone with me in this Venusberg?'

'It worries me to know why we're here. Any clandestine meeting around here would be strictly for one end and that non-political and do you have to go on calling me "Harree", when any pick-up would have to be mounted in a blue-bell?'

Xenia looked hurt. 'I have to get eento the part. You don't appreciate me. Do you think I *laike* spending an afternoon with a great, cold Earthworm? We walk along by the shore. Then we must cross to the island. That ees where they meet. At night thees place ees veray busee. All leet up with coloured lights and they have fireworks. Eet was not so easy then, I can tell you.'

He could imagine it. Working alone in the semi-dark, liable to be taken as fair game by any pleasure seeker, she must have needed an iron nerve.

He said, 'I take it back. Call me "Harree" as much as you think necessary. How do we get across as of now?'

'We sweem.'

Fletcher thought, ' Ask a silly question and you get a silly answer,' but it was clearer as they followed the edge of the lake. Heavily indented with tiny coves, it was a natural for semi-private bathing parties. Four hundred metres of picking a devious path through preoccupied couples and they made out to a narrow promontory which ran towards the island.

When they reached its tip, Xenia kicked off her sandals and dabbled her feet in the water.

A Garamasian pair, who had been swimming and were drying off in the tropical heat, looked at them with blank, incurious stares. Xenia, who had the Fingalnian unconcern about nudity, stared back. Fletcher, even after recent conditioning, felt a prickle of discomfort under his mask.

Xenia said, 'Harree, thees water ees lovelee. We should take a sweem.'

If it was a handout for Garamasian ears, the obsidian eye disks showed no interest. Ongoing action gave the text a running illustration. Xenia had her tabard off and was wriggling athletically out of minimal apricot briefs before Fletcher could get a warning past his epiglottis.

He need not have worried. Skin treatment in a pale coffee tan had been carried out on a full-figure basis and when she turned round to say, 'Hurree, Harree,' he could see that frontal treatment had been engineered by the same careful hand. She was still European on all counts.

Dag Fletcher took a moment off to consider that in all the vagaries of service commitment, he had not been on any more bizarre mission and wondered where along the line he could have made a stand. Certainly not at this point. He left his city gent's outfit in a tidy pile and followed slowly into the water.

It was clear and warm shelving rapidly to a uniform two-metre depth, where the mauve plant-life gave way to glass-smooth green clay and outcrops of white marble. He caught up with Xenia and swam alongside.

'I take it your dye stays fast.'

'Eet needs som special solvent to take eet off. Just relax Harree and enjoy yourself.'

She flicked a palm-sized gobbet of lake water into his open mouth and dived like an eel. Fletcher whacked down hard on her neat buttocks before they disappeared and dived in pursuit.

He found her on a white plinth, a drowned figurine with black hair floating up in a spiral eddy and for a count of three, they considered each other, faces only centimetres apart. He was getting a new slant on the Fingalnan psyche. At least *this* example of it. Group judgements were always wrong. Maybe there was no such animal as the national type, beloved of sociometrics. Only individuals. Eyes looking out on the world as his own did.

Though even conceding that, you had to admit that Scotians were all of a piece. But then they were specially trained for the military role, like Spartans of another age and they hardly classified as human. Something had been left out of the biological kit.

All this camaraderie and tough professionalism of Xenia's now? Good qualities, but how would she rate as an individual? Where would her loyalties finally lie? To a friend or to the system?

For that matter his own position was left with a question mark at the centre. In the last analysis, he would be hard put to it to know which way he would choose between individual values and the I.G.O. code which he had accepted on oath.

Overhead, the surface was a corrugated aluminium roof. Xenia grinned showing even, white teeth and launched herself upwards, brushing his face with satin-smooth thighs. Then she settled down to a steady, purposeful crawl.

When he caught up again, she said, 'Well, Harree, you will just have to wait and see what I do. Let us hope we nevaire have to make thees choice.'

It was clear enough that water was no barrier to communication. She had followed its private argument at least on the main count.

On the island, heavy vegetation ran down to the water line. It had been planted out to be a landscape feature in the lake. They crawled ashore into a hot yellow twilight and two metres from the lake could stand erect, screened from the shore.

Again, he marvelled that she had come here alone in the dark. Whatever else, she had formidable will power. Silversilk over steel.

Currently, professionalism was raising its head. There was no element of banter, when she said shortly, 'Thees way,' and led into the wood.

It was a trim back to follow through any grove and the pay off came as an anticlimax.

54

Twenty metres on she stopped dead and he had to fend off from smooth shoulders, slippery with sweat. Dead ahead was an overgrown clearing. Instead of a gothic folly, which would have fitted the script, the complex of small buildings in the centre was square and functional. Angle-framed with grey corrugated cladding. A two-floor oblong in the centre, with lean-to extensions on every face. The nearest was partly glazed and filled with a jumble of empty seed trays.

Xenia said, 'I observed eet for som time. Eet ees always emptee at thees hour. Later the park workers prepare for firework deesplay on the lake.'

Fletcher felt very vulnerable. Every military precept told him that he should have fire cover at his back before crossing an open space. But Xenia was already running lightly for the nearest blank wall.

So far, it was as she said. Ear to the hot cladding he listened for a count of ten. Nothing stirred. He nodded and they went on.

Round the far side, there was a paved slipway and the square transom of a long boat lying on chocks on an eight-wheeled trolley poked out from the miniature jungle.

Double-leaf doors, with deep ventilation louvres gave access to the building. Xenia went further on to a small window set high in the wall. It was obvious what she intended and Fletcher stood with his back to it and made a stirrup to lift her over his head.

She was feather light. Close enough to see the fine grain of her skin and check out an identity symbol in the soft crease of her groin, a small star-shaped silver mole which had not reacted to the dye treatment.

Then he was alone for half a minute, until she had made her way through the inside to open the main door.

Round aluminium bins were stacked in tiers. A long work

55

bench was littered with card cylinders, where the park staff had been preparing for the evening session. Boxes of finished fireworks stood ready for loading on the boat. On one wall, a framework made up for a finale tableau was leaned in metre wide sections for easy handling.

In the centre, an open aluminium ladder led aloft to top deck. Xenia signalled for up, with an expressive forefinger and mounted the narrow treads like any cat.

Fletcher followed more slowly. Long habit of weighing a situation in military terms made him cautious. There was no escape route. If she had miscalculated the time or some eager-beaver groundsman appeared early for his stint, they would be cut off.

Xenia had shoved away a hinged trap with a nice contraction of gluteal muscle for the chore. Head level with the back of her knees, he heard her quick intake of breath, before she was plucked through the hole.

There was no time to make a judgement. He was heaving himself after her with a total mobilization of power, before he could decide whether the true strategy would have been to get out, while there was half a chance.

He whipped up into a dim light. There could have been a circle of patient fishers round the seal hole, but in fact there had been only one, a short, barrel-chested Laodamian, ungainly in a gavotte, but custom built for this exercise. Xenia had clamped herself to his chest like a poultice and was in process of being choked. Only frenetic rolling of the head had stopped the man finding the right pressure point.

Fletcher took him behind, chopping into his thick neck with linked hands. Even then it was touch and go whether the fingers on Xenia's windpipe answered the blacked out brain before they had done their work.

Fletcher kept the composite bundle upright and prised them

56

loose one at a time. She fell away and for his money could be dead. His immediate problem was how to make a lasting impression on a smooth hairless head with the thickest bone structure in the galaxy, a flat spread nose of pure gristle and deeply recessed eye sockets.

A Laodamian. That figured. As well as being ahead on mind control techniques, they were as suggestible as Pavlov's dog. Once talked into it, they had a tolerance for long vigils that would send any other human type cafard. He backed his zombie to the nearest wall and slammed its head on a handy cross-girder.

Xenia lay where she had dropped. Before he went near, he checked round the set.

It was stacked with metre-cube crates with only a rough, clear oblong round the stair head. Along one wall there was evidence that some unpacking had been done. Maybe units had been assembled and despatched elsewhere. An overhead hoist powered by a small linear motor running on a T-beam led to a sliding panel on the rear outer wall and showed how the gear had been swung in. Heavy merchandize at that. It coud not have been imported without the say-so of many Garamasian officials.

On the other hand, the island maintenance centre was a good cover. Consignments of powder would be regularly shipped across.

He followed round every wall and walked through every alley between the rows of crates. There was nobody else. They were alone. Or he was alone. He went back to the stairhead and knelt down beside the girl.

Some cynic had said that the most frightening thing in his book was the false complacency of a sleeping face. Xenia's was smooth and regular as a mask. He straightened her out and put his ear to her chest. There was a precise and regular beat.

Lying beside the nearer crates was a low bed on trestles covered with rugs. She would be more comfortable on that while he took a look at what the crates held.

Skin was warm and resilient. Hands and feet very delicate. When he put her down, he spent a minute arranging her borrowed hair in a symmetrical fan and leaned over with a hand on either side of her head. He imagined her without the make-up. A very remarkable piece of biological engineering. The small, silver princess of a Scandinavian folk tale, unexpectedly made flesh; but tough as high-tensile steel.

She spoke without opening her eyes and he knew she had been conscious for some time, long enough, anyway, to beam in on that last thought sequence. 'You killed the dragon, too, Harree. You should claim the standard reward. Or does your Earth type sense of proprietee rule eet out?'

Fletcher knew he was dodging a decision which would have to be faced again, 'As of now, we have work to do. Get yourself out of bed and check out the gorilla. See if he has anything useful. I'll open a crate and take a look. Hurry it up. There's a time line on that car. Also, in spite of your delightful company, I'd like to get some clothes on.'

'I can see that might begeen to worree you. But I am broadminded. You don't have to mind about me.'

'Just get a wriggle on.'

In the end it was Xenia who became anxious about the time. Having nothing to do except watch, she was more conscious of it.

Working quickly and methodically Fletcher opened six crates in turn, carefully repacking every item as he finished with it, storing away detail in his mind and getting Xenia to look at pieces of equipment which her memory could help to identify.

In the end, he was satisfied. Without knowing precisely the form of the finished product, he could say that over the six crates there was enough duplication to build three sets. At a rough count there would be thirty crates.

Whatever it was, had a short range and needed repeaters or numerous broadcast points.

Eyes unfocused in speculation, he found he was looking at Xenia across a small mound of equipment. She was squatting unselfconsciously, knees apart with a straight back, a powerful retinal image that had made its impact like a subliminal stimulus. Suggestion below the threshold of consciousness. That was what the equipment was all about.

'What ees eet, Harree? Have you feeneeshed with thees? We must go.'

'You gave me an idea.'

'There's no time now. You had your chance. Even thees Earth type feection does not offaire a reward twice,'

'You have a one-track mind Xenia. Get this stuff back. I have something to do down below.'

When she joined him, he had the Laodamian crumpled realistically at the foot of the ladder. Like Elpenor, on another island, he had clearly missed his footing and taken a short cut to oblivion.

Trailing round the room in a rough spiral, Fletcher had eased out a length of twisted paper fuse, leading it, for the lay-off to an open keg.

He said, 'All straight upstairs?'

'Yes.'

There was no need to check. If she said so, it was okay. He recognized that she was the ideal lieutenant for a mission. In spite of appearances, nothing would be overlooked or neglected. She would make a good co-pilot. Except that the effect on the crew would be ambivalent.

'Ready then?'

'Yes.'

He took a blaster from the dead Laodamian's side pouch and shot carefully at the end of the fuse.

Outside the door he heard her methodically fixing it as it had been, then the quick pad of feet to the window. He was there to swing her down and they ran hand in hand for the bush.

'How long weell eet take?'

'Ten maybe twelve minutes.'

They crawled out into the lake and swam underwater for ten metres. Then Xenia streaked ahead in a racing crawl that was difficult to hold.

At the promontory, the Garamasian couple had moved into the shallows to replay the score in another medium and took no noticed as they dressed and moved off up the hill at a deceptively casual saunter.

At the top, Xenia said, 'I should have stopped you. Eeet ees always a meestake to be too clevaire. Eef you had left heem, eet would have been enough. Now they weell *know* that some-one has seen the equeepment. Your fusee has gone out.'

Fletcher believed it himself. He kept the admission out of positive thought, in case she was doing a radar scan. It was, in its way, humiliating to be an open book. Also, she had the right of it. He had been carried away by a piece of military thinking that was not appropriate to the espionage role. De-strucion of potential enemy installations was not the mission. He should have been content to report back with the flash of insight which had been triggered off by Xenia's taut pose.

A white plume jetted from the centre of the island, followed by a percussive thud and a ground tremor that dislodged small stones from the hill. An instant tidal wave built in an expanding circle.

Orange and vermilion flame unfolded an intense asterisk over the site. Banshee howls signalled take off for special effects rockets, which streaked out every which way.

All over the park, couples sat up to confirm that it was not a textbook subjective phenomenon.

Xenia said handsomely, 'I take eet all back, Harree. You were right and I was wrong. Nevairetheless, we should get the hell out of eet, I theenk.'

MOVING alone in the corridors of the Space Centre Hotel, Fletcher felt isolated. It was something he should have gotten used to, after the years in space service; but right now the contrast of the filled and unfilled interval was stronger than any time he could remember. Nothing scheduled until the midmorning meeting with Duvorac.

He had left Xenia in a busy quarter and made his own way by auto shuttle to the I.G.O. penthouse car port. He had left, after a quick session in the changing room and put in an aimless stint round a shopping precinct. Two bulky parcels, elaborately gift-wrapped proved it.

At his door, he searched clumsily for a pass key, until he saw he was squandering time. It was open.

Mind still half off load in a bid to evaluate Xenia against all previous notions of the female idea, he looked at it in simple surprise and went ahead without any expectation of danger.

He was framed in the opening, a plumb target for any amateur assassin, before the full impact fell. As an undercover agent he was a bad risk.

In the event, it was a good entrance. Professional caution would have looked out of character. In peripheral vision, he picked out two guards, back against the walls on either side. Pedasun, sitting on the only easy chair, twiddling a yellow cane, watched him in and made no effort to stand in honour of the host.

He did speak. Something pithy in Garamasian and the left hand marker moved smartly to close the door and stood with his back to it.

Fletcher went on walking, conscious of a cold area in the centre of his spine. He dumped his treasure trove on a bedside table and said, 'Colonel Pedasun, isn't it? You should let me know when you want to call. You might have had a long wait.'

Pedasun spoke again and the right hand man who had been standing at ease, snapped into action. He unhitched a syringe gun from his tunic belt and lined it up on Fletcher's chest, a target he could not miss at the range. His partner circled round outside the line of fire.

Switching to English, Pedasun said, 'You will have no objection to a check for arms?'

'And if I have?'

'You would be unwise. A single shot of tranquillizer and there would be no choice at all.'

'I remind you that I am an accredited I.G.O. officer.'

'That is a point; but a minor one. You are still required to obey Garamasian law. If I take you to my headquarters, which I might decide to do, the I.G.O. authority will not interfere. They are realists. They would not strain political relations for one man.'

Fletcher said, 'There is no need. I carry no weapons.'

'Very well. I accept that. You see, I am a very reasonable man. I can see you have been buying gifts. What else have you been doing?'

'As you will know, I am waiting for a posting to a new ship. I spend some time each day at I.G.O. Headquarters. Other than that, time drags. I shall be glad of employment.'

'You have already had some. You visited the internment area. That visit coincided with an unusual demonstration. Also, a Fingalnan girl, waiting for identification, took the opportunity to break out. Today there was an unusual disturbance at the Stymphalus Park. Two Earth citizens were noticed there. One a tall man; one, a small woman. Could it be that you were there?'

Fletcher said, 'I have no idea how many Earth nationals are in Kristinobyl; but it must run to some thousands, why should you ask me that question?'

'That is not a satisfactory answer.'

'Conceding that you have any right to ask questions, I will say that I would find it difficult to prove that I was anywhere at all. I roam about a good deal. No, I was not at your park.'

'Since you are unsure in general terms, why are you so sure you were not there?'

'That's a reasonable point; but I would remember a park.'

'Well we shall see.' Pedasun spoke again in Garamasian and a guard crossed the foot of the bed to the washroom. Whipping back the door, with the air of one who operates a trick cabinet, he enlarged the symposium by two. Garamasians both. A man and a woman.

They could have been any two frightened people; but Pedasun cued in recall. 'Come forward. Do you recognize this Earthman as the one who left clothes near you and swam across to the island?'

They were clearly in a dilemma. Agreement would please Pedasun; but a session on a truth couch in a courtroom would show up any uncertainty and spoil his case. Disappointment now might be safer.

The man had difficulty keeping his voice steady. Whatever he said was too long for yes and hand gestures were describing a different kind of face.

64

Pedasun tried the woman, she tripped over her tongue, coughed extensively in mid exposition and then stepped back behind her escort.

Watching Pedasun's face, Fletcher could see he was struggling with a decision. Silence deepened round the set. The girl hiccupped suddenly and covered her face with her hands. The next smooth talker with a proposition for an afternoon by the lakeside was going to hit opposition.

Pedasun lifted himself slowly from his chair and whacked it a couple of times with his swagger cane, as a compensatory activity for what was on his mind. 'So Commander, it appears that you are right. They do not identify you. It is fortunate, for your sake. But I advise you to be careful. There is something about you which instinct tells me is not right. I have a nose for intrigue. I can smell it out.'

Changing tone, he spoke rapidly in patois and the room cleared in a count of three.

Fletcher lit a cigarette and took it out on his balcony. First reaction was to call Duvorac; but then Pedasun had been in the suite for some time. He would have it on some subtle link for a sure thing. An agent's lot was rough. It needed a special type of outlook which he did not have. There was infinite responsibility without an atom of power to beat a way through. Sometimes in his corvette, he judged he had been stuck with a near-impossible mission; but then there was megapower under his thumb and knowledge that the ongoing situation could be met at a personal level.

Here, he was everybody's hey-you, with the added insult that once inside Pedasun's brig nobody would want to know.

Suddenly he felt restless. The next thirty hours, even allowing for a ration of sleep were like an endless desert to cross. He walked over to the video. Yola had given him a number to call. What would Pedasun make of this? Nothing good. Better to go in person.

Positive action worked its therapy. Looking out over Kristinobyl, he saw it in a new light. Somebody had to look out for the patient millions. Not only here either. All over the galaxy there were centres of population dependent for continuing peace on the devious work of I.G.O. personnel. Men like Duvorac who accepted a long and thankless discomfort to serve an idea. What people did with their peace when they had it was irrelevant.

He saw for truth the proposition that all generations are equidistant from barbarism. The whole structure of civilized man was a house of cards tottering in a draught. He had no right to drag his feet on any mission that helped to shore up the foundations.

God, any minute now, he would be saluting the flag. He poured himself a drink, took it into the shower and held it outside the spray. Five minutes later, he was in the express elevator for reception carrying one of his parcels. It would make some kind of pretext for visiting Yola.

Fletcher reached the lobby of the female students' residential block, after a zig-zag course which had tested out his skills as a navigator. In the end, he was sure that he was followed and he watched the swing doors to see who it would be.

It was, in fact, a young Garamasian male, not in uniform but having the aura of one, who came through. He carried a bulky black zip case, looked everywhere except at him and then settled for an alcove with a newsreader, as though waiting for an RV on his own account.

The clerk at the kiosk, an ageing matron with a disapproving voice, obligingly identified the first caller. 'You can go up,

Commander Fletcher, Room 61, third level. Visits to residents must not exceed fifteen minutes except in the common room. Check here as you leave.'

If Venus hated haste as she was reputed to do, that would be tough on some. Though there was always Stymphalus Park as a fallback.

Yola's pad was small, but well-equipped. A composite dressing chest and work console filled the right hand wall. Facing the door, a wall-to-wall solar window gave light and heat. On the left a pale oblong panel marked the site of the truckle bed which had been swung away to give clear space. There was one easy chair, finished in bronze metal cloth and a rack of technical manuals.

She was working at the desk and said over her shoulder, 'Excuse me for two minutes, Commander. I have to finish this. Please sit down.'

The tone was not friendly and he conceded that she had a point. Also, if she was down in Pedasun's book, the room might be monitored.

Two minutes was nearer five, before she went into the end game and typed rapidly on the keyboard. When the output went into a spasm and delivered a long tape to her hand, she shoved back a swathe of hair, sighed heavily and swivelled her chair to face the guest.

Fletcher said, 'Not working out?'

'No. But I see where the error is. It won't take long to fix.'

'I called for two things. I was at the internment centre when a crowd of students showed up. Some were hurt I believe. I wanted to see if you were okay. Also, I hope to be leaving fairly soon and we won't need your excellent services as an interpreter. Here's a small thank-you token. You were very helpful.

Black obsidean disks gave him a straight look. She had

67

latched on to his reason for caution. A small nod towards the video confirmed it. There was also something else in the background which he could not fathom.

'Is there not a saying in your country—fear the Greeks bearing gifts?'

'You only have to worry about that if they give you a horse.'

'Then I suppose I should say thank you. I am not happy today. Several of my friends were killed. It was a cruel business.'

'Aren't you going to open it?'

'Oh yes. I am sorry to be discourteous.' Again there was a quick look which seemed to be searching for ulterior motives. Maybe it was a standard gambit for a proposition.

When it was standing on the preparation tray of her console, she had a more genuine reaction. 'That's lovely, Commander. I shall enjoy having it in my room.'

It was a large vacuum bell on a copper plinth. Inside, three non-friction rings ran in an endless complicated pattern on each other's rims. An engineer's abstract.

Yola watched it for a minute, then appeared to come to a decision. 'I will walk down to reception with you.'

Two paces outside the door, she said in a fierce whisper, 'Did you *know* what would happen to us. We are not fools. You *used* us for some purpose of your own. Why did you come?'

There was enough truth in it to leave a bitter taste, but there was no time for a long defence. He did say, however, 'You are partly right, but believe me I had no idea you would be harmed. I would like you to take me to one of your group meetings. There is a new danger, which you are not aware of. In this, you are helping me; but to a far greater degree helping yourselves.'

'Why should I trust you?'

'That's a good question. I can only say that you must. It is more important than you can know.'

'I will think about it and find some way to let you know. But do not be too sure of us.'

She turned back at the elevator, obviously anxious to avoid being booked for fraternization with a discredited alien.

In the lobby, Fletcher was half way to the door when he changed course and walked over to the Garamasian, who was zipping up his brief case ready to leave.

He leaned confidentially on the back of his settle and used basic speech tones, 'If you are going my way, we could use the same shuttle and save expense all round.'

Courtesy made no friends. For a short space, the man struggled with a vocabulary problem and a sure knowledge that the higher echelons would not be pleased. Finally he gritted out, 'No. No thank you. I have my own transport. It is not necessary.'

'Well I'll say goodnight then. Joy in your life.'

Facial evidence suggested that there was not much in the forseeable future.

In his own shuttle, Fletcher reckoned he had been unwise. To justify himself, the man might be that much tougher with Yola. But the manifest would show that their conversation had no loaded element. They would have checked with her anyway after the visit.

He half expected that Pedasun would be back in his room for another conference; but it was empty and suddenly inhospitable. He had a nostalgia for the ward room of a ship and the conversation of his own kind. Even the presence of his own people without conversation for that matter, would be all gain. Though he had to admit, in sober truth, that there was as much likelihood of being out of key with a group of

Earthmen as anybody else. When you got right down to it, communication was in short supply all round. There was nobody on exactly the same wavelength.

Xenia could be, if she chose. But that would be by a positive adjustment on her part. She was not naturally sympathetic.

He spent some time watching a traditional drama on the actualizer in the nearest common room. Its arcane symbolism was strictly for Garamasian nationals and even with a language cracker delivering an English text to his left ear, he could make nothing out of it. So he went early to bed, following the precept that he who has nothing may sleep, with the drapes back and a brilliant star map over the balcony rail.

Fletcher came wide awake searching the ceiling overhead for the illuminated tell-tale which gave him the ship's course before he moved.

Tactile clues flooded in. The wide bed and the texture of the furnishings, cued him to the here and now. He was ashore.

But some alarm had gone off in his head. Recall established it as a soft thud, as though a padded cosh had tapped a solid surface. He rolled out of the sack and stood up in one smooth flow. There was enough starlight to see that the room was empty. He unplugged an angle-poise table light from beside the bed and shoved it under the covers. With the shade on the pillow and the covers plumped out, it gave the rough semblance of a sleeping man.

The wash room was on an interior wall. No entrance there except round the twist. The iris-eye door could only be either open or closed and it was shut. It had to be the balcony.

Eyes adjusted to the dark, he went along the rail. In the left hand corner there was a thickening, a smudge of darkness on darkness. Some climber-upward had lodged a grapnel.

What was he waiting for? If the room was monitored, they could amplify the breathing rhythms of a sleeping man.

He forced himself to breath slow and deep, as though he had resettled after an uneasy spell.

Still working at it, he moved over to beside the door and flattened to the wall with the bed and the balcony in view.

Over the rail, the night sky had a cinnamon tinge that magnified the stars in a staggered recession into infinity. Somewhere out there, the squadron was on its endless patrol. Where he ought to be, for godsake, instead of in this rats' alley.

Three minutes passed, time for endless vision and revision; but he filled it keeping a check on tension and concentrating on the area above the grab.

When a dark silhouette rose waist high over the bar, it was so inevitable and expected that his breathing rhythm was unchanged.

From the bulk, it was likely to be a Laodamian. The shape, having grown, stabilized, shoulders hunched behind the slim barrel of a gun, there was a soft plop and a jerk in the bunched fabric on the bed. Fletcher stopped breathing. The man waited, leaned forward, watchful, then diminished smoothly in size until he was gone. Still holding his breath, Fletcher put finger tips to the door panel and eased it away.

Outside, there were dim courtesy lights on the corridor and he checked his time disk. Three hundred hours on the nose. Nobody was likely to be around except the all-night clerk in the lobby. He padded along to the landing at the stairhead where there was a small lounge area with a balcony on the same side as his own.

Lights were still on here and there in a random pattern along the cliff face of the hotel. Counting forward, he identified his own room and checked immediately below. The only balcony in direct line was two floors down. As he watched, there was a pale glow that snapped on and off again as an inner door opened and closed.

He gave it half an hour sitting in shadow in a deep club chair. Then he went back to his room. It was pointless to try to find the pick up. But then, they would be satisfied. Nobody would go on listening to a silence.

He cleared the bed and found a small circular splash of bright yellow serum on the unbreakable lamp shade. Most of his gear was in the I.G.O. consulate and he travelled light. A handgrip took the rest. Except his remaining gift parcel which he shoved under his arm. It was like clearing up after a death. Twenty minutes later, he was checking in at a cosmopolitan rooming house in a quiet square in Kristinobyl.

Duvorac said, 'You are sure, Commander, that you were not seen leaving the Space Centre and that you stayed out of sight until you came here?'

'Quite sure.'

'In spite of your reservations, it could be that you have missed your vocation. You have the makings of an agent.'

'I wouldn't bank on that.'

'Nevertheless you must be giving the opposition a great deal to think about. Now as to the equipment. What would be its use?'

'Only an electronics expert could establish that.'

'But Xenia tells me that you formed an opinion.'

'More of a hunch.'

Xenia following the exchange like a tennis umpire, put in helpfully, 'He got eet by looking at me.'

Duvorac with heavy gallantry, but some justice, said, 'I am

72

sure you give food for vision to a great variety of ethnic types, but go on, Commander.'

'The apparatus is not self-powered and would have a limited range. But a large number of units, well-sited could cover a population centre. They would use power from the ring. I believe it is a device for sub-liminal projection, so that public opinion could be manipulated. That would explain O.G.A. interest. We destroyed some, but many may be already in position. It would be the ideal set-up to prepare for a *coup*.'

Duvorac's console chattered into independent life and he consulted a message tape. He took a spell to read it off and Xenia filled the interval with, 'I was sure you were in some dangaire last night. I felt eet here.'

A slim hand pointed delicately to her chest, only notionally covered by lime-green net. 'Eet was about three o'clock and I woke up. But I knew you were veree clevaire and would be all right. At four o'clock I knew you were safe and went to sleep again.'

So he had not been totally out on a limb in his corner of space. He tried to fathom what was behind her eyes. Except that they were green in depth and very subtle developments of the genre, there was no progress to be made.

He was still working at it, when Duvorac broke silence and the commissar had to start again, 'If I could have your attention for a moment, Commander. The occupant of the room below yours checked out early. He was a Laodamian, Melas by name. First officer of a freighter which is due out at noon. There is no doubt, the O.G.A. nationals here have a close organization. Headquarters will be at one of the consulates. They will have the same diplomatic immunity as ourselves. Without unshakable evidence, we can take no action.'

'Next time you should arrange to catch one actually shoving a knife in my back.'

'I hope that will not be necessary,'—Duvorac said it as though he did not rule it out, but would only use the idea if pushed and Fletcher reckoned that there was some force in the old gag that a man might regret speech, but seldom regretted silence.

There was a digestive pause and Duvorac, having considered the angles, went on, 'I judge that you should return to your new quarters and wait until the girl Yola makes contact. I will see that she knows where you are. Her friends are well placed to find out where power is taken from the ring. If you could bring one of the devices here, it could be analysed by our technicians and a counter move would be possible.'

'If you have jamming in mind, it's not on. These are small high-power jobs, widely spread, building an intense local field.'

'Then we must have them located and give proof to the government of what is intended. They can then deal with the problem.'

'Is that a serious proposal?'

'Of course, Commander. I am always serious.'

'But the government is riddled with sympathizers. Action would be delayed, maybe blocked altogether. By the time they moved, the broadcasts could be in full spate and then action would be influenced by the very agent it was trying to suppress. We wouldn't get to first base relying on Garamasian action.'

'What do you suggest?'

It dawned on Fletcher that he had been nicely angled round into the position of a fellow planner. Once a scheme had been agreed, he would be morally obliged to go along with it.

Xenia, who had been on a seemingly-random roaming kick round the office, gravitated to a spot at the back of his chair and he could feel the heat exchange going on, as her metabolism maintained her at a body heat five degrees over the Earth figure.

But he had been asked a legitimate question and it demanded an answer. When it came, he wondered whether her mental fingers had been shifting a few keys in the computer.

He listened to himself saying, 'There is only one sure way, and it would be effective at several levels. We should send a cutting out party into one of the remote areas, where the power ring is accessible, and sabotage it. Make a break that would take weeks to fix. That would prevent broadcasts for a period, give them time to pinpoint the transmitters, and take off some of the attraction of Garamas for O.G.A. purposes. It's the power source that pulls them.'

Xenia was close up behind him and put her head against his right ear, a warm, silk fragrance, rather than a physical touch. 'You are clevaire, Harree. That is a splendeed idea. The commissar ees nonplussed.'

True or false, Duvorac rallied gamely. A lifetime of indirect action made an open gambit hard for him to judge. He shifted about on his plinth and said, 'That is the military way, of course. You would naturally think along those lines. The scheme has a lot to recommend it. I will think about it and discuss it with Admiral Varley. It would require precise and accurate timing and would have to be arranged so that no hint of suspicion fell on I.G.O. Many people would suffer hardship. It could harden opinion against us. Indeed to coin a phrase, we could be hoist with our own petard.'

He stopped transmitting and went into a contemplative phase. Xenia still up close whispered, 'What ees thees petard, Harree? I theenk I nevaire saw one.'

'You didn't miss a thing, and for godsake stop calling me Harree, it's confusing.'

'But I like Harree. You *suit* Harree. Thees Dag ees too

75

short and sharp. Harree ees more leengereeng and loveeng. That perfume jar was a Harree-geeft, eef evaire I saw one.'

Duvorac who had ignored the pillow talk like any blind fiddler, stirred into speech.

'This needs time to consider. I will meet you again at this time tomorrow. Make a detailed plan of where you consider the ring could be broken. Xenia will bring any further instructions, if I have them.'

In Fletcher's experience, ordinary citizens in Kristinobyl were either positively friendly or indifferent. Filling time in the market place, a packed rabbit-warren of temporary stalls, which had appeared overnight in the square outside his window, he slowly became conscious that attitudes could go sour. He had sensed a lack of *rapport* in one or two Omphalian stall keepers, when he went under their awnings to take a closer look at the tourist gew-gaws on offer.

Omphalians were the natural-born traders of the galaxy. They would and did sell anything that could be picked up and moved to anyone with negotiable assets. Barter was a way of life. When they backed away without making a pitch as from a leper bell, there had to be a reason.

Confirmation came when a small Garamasian child, finding him near, sent up a high-pitched wail and ran to its mother.

Every eye on the set, and they were a mixed lot, tracked round to stare at him as though he had been foiled in a bid to snatch its lolly.

The over-riding impression was that it only went to prove a point, Earth nationals were beyond the human pale.

He went on down the alley between open booths and felt the weight of disfavour like a psychokinetic force beating on the back of his head.

Weaving left and right he cleared the child-protecting group, but the new crowd was no better.

He found himself rationalizing the experience. After all, why should an Earthman be welcome? For the most part they were only seen following an I.G.O. mandate. They brought not peace, but a sword. Comfortable ways had to be given up. And who was to judge the justice of that? If a custom, however barbarous was okay to the people concerned who had any right to knock it?

He was in the area of absolute standards. When you got in that thicket, you could only say—it is right, because it seems right to me.

Earthman go home—about summed it up. In fact, the slogan came before his mind's eye in banner headlines and triggered off an alarm. If he was thinking that way, there was no surprise that others should go one farther on.

Somewhere in the area, they must be giving a Laodamian opinion manipulator its trial run. Pedasun's fine Italian hand could have set the text so as to waste no drop of bile. Xenophobia would be a strong prop in any fascist programme.

Intellectually, there was some satisfaction in having sorted the angles; but it was likely to be the only clear gain to be had. From being passive critics, the more suggestible elements of the *hoi polloi* began to pack together and form a lynch mob.

He had gotten himself towards the centre of the square and there was no escape route except through the cordon.

Now he knew what it was like to be Ishmael.

All the women and children had disappeared. Solid wedges of young Garamasian men were coming in from either end of the alley he was in. Some of them had picked up lengths of scantling and were swinging them clubwise. From being a hive of demented chat, the whole square had gone silent.

Running would trigger off a chase, he walked slowly under

the nearest awning and then vaulted over the counter. A small, fat Omphalian, greasy spheroid, topped with lank, black hair, let out a yell thinking it was a heist.

It was a signal for pandemonium to break out. Fletcher cut across another stall, but he might have been carrying a homing signal, groups formed ahead of him at every turn. He grabbed a basketwork lid from a linen coffer, a knob-ended chair leg from a do-it-yourself furniture kit and began to run down an alley that led direct for the hotel.

A stone thudded home between his shoulder-blades. Men appeared blocking his path. From a simple exercise of getting clear, he was fighting to survive.

In some ways, numbers were against them. He was the only one who knew who was on his side. A dozen blows that could have killed him were blocked in the press.

He was two-thirds through and reckoned he would make it, getting the balance of his chair leg and swinging it like a mace, when the open end of the gully filled with another party which had made a flanking move. He knew he had to stay on his feet. But there was a fifth column working in his head trying to sell the idea that he was in the wrong.

Backed up against a post, he cleared a swathe in front and missed the Laodamian who crawled under the counter to grab his ankles. As he pitched forward the crowd surged in from every side.

A shrewd knock over his left ear, clouded vision in a red haze. In a last spasm of effort, he kicked his legs free and rolled convulsively under the counter of the stall, before his mind rolled away from him in a free-wheeling trip into black space.

CHAPTER FIVE

IN the Command cabin of *Europa*, Garamas was plate-size on the main scanner; a cinnamon-tinged sphere banded by white vapour.

Admiral P. J. Varley, thick-set, greying, with an underslung pirhana jaw, currently clamped shut to give support to a black briar pipe, focussed boiled blue eyes on it. Even through the aromatic smoke screen he was sending up, the planet had no *charisma*.

He was sick of Garamas and the problems it posed. In many respects an out-and-out hostile would be easier to handle.

Shifting irritably out of his executive console on the command island, he stumped over to a raised observation platform that followed the quadrant curve of a panoramic, direct vision port.

The view was no great improvement. When you had said it was different you had said all.

Outside the gravisphere of Garamas, he had brought the squadron down on the black cinder heap of a burned out asteroid. Light from the ships threw up a nightmare landscape of tumbled basalt and pumice dust. Criss-cross of slender shadows of five towering ships. Silver obelisks in a bizarre grove. Backdrop for a demoniac rite of passage.

Fresh crews would be under stress to maintain station, day

after day in this limbo. Coming at the tail end of a gruelling mission, it was the last twist of the screw.

Captains' daily logs featured mounting infringements of service regs. Varley, staring through a ghost image of himself on the glass reckoned that the only crime he was not going to hear of was desertion. Whatever jigs a latter-day Bligh got up to, the pressure would never force a man outside into that mind-numbing desolation.

Not that any of his commanders was likely to go cafard and have crewmen holy-stoning the deck. He reviewed them in his mind's eye. Simpson of *Falcon*, dark, with a predatory, hook-nose, a natural born sailor for any age; Driscoll of *Heron*, ox-solid, nothing would get under his skin; Cameron, the huge, raw-boned Scot, commanding *Hawk,* a nerveless, tireless machine; *Drake*'s commander, Cooper, round-faced, cherubic, resilient as latex. No. They would hold the pass for a time yet. Though it was up to himself to see that it was not too long.

The hatch at his back slid aside. *Europa*'s captain, Group Commander Frazer, ducked in under the lintel, a tall fair man with hair clipped so short that he seemed prematurely bald and, by contrast, his face looked over youthful and immature —an error which had trapped many a new crewman into thinking he would be easy. A short-lived miscalculation at that.

Varley said, 'I'll give it three more days, Bob. Then we pull out. I've seen this before. A revolution that's expected any day can hang off for years. I do believe there's a revolutionary type that likes the intrigue bit. Doesn't want to take responsibility. Never grows up.'

'What about *Petrel,* Admiral?' Do we leave her for the relieving squadron?'

'For godsake why should we do that? There'll be an official

visit for Blue Squadron to present credentials. They can make their own arrangements for putting a toad in the hole.'

'What about Fletcher?'

'Publish the enquiry. Let him bring *Petrel* out with the skeleton crew.'

'Will you tell him why the enquiry was held up?'

'Not immediately. He's a good man, but it'll do him no harm to sweat a little. He thinks he knows it all.'

'It paid off. He was useful to Duvorac.'

'Working for the civilian arm will be good experience. If he stays with the service, he should know how their minds run. Get a signal off telling Duvorac I want him back.'

A calling bleep drew both men to look at the signals desk. Communications had done a good job centring a Venusian face, twice life-size on the middle panel. Overhead a tannoy said, 'Call from I.G.O. Commissar, Garamas, sir. Urgent. Using scrambled link. Will you take it, sir?'

Varley said, 'Holy cow. Did you ever hear of Venusians being long-distance mind-readers? What does the old fox want do you think?'

From the vantage point of some years close partnership, Frazer made a bid for progress, 'I suggest you ask him, Admiral. Shall I stay?'

'Yes, you'd better know.'

Varley sat down at his desk and flipped a succession of keys to put himself in circuit with speech, vision, scrambler, decode and interpreter services. Then he said, flatly, 'Varley. What can I do for you Commissar?'

The voice that made out through the intricate metallic gut, matched oddly with the Venusian's massive grey face. It was a lightweight female job, on the high-pitched side; but it delivered a plain tale in plain terms.

When Duvorac paused to rest his larynx, Varley was up to

date on the scene. He said 'So you believe, Commissar, that the crisis is imminent and we should act to sabotage the ring. You understand that any ship, sidestepping Garamas control, for a planetfall anywhere outside Kristinobyl, would be a justifiable target for defence action. Unless I neutralized ground installations first, it would not get within a thousand kilometres. That would mean devastation for every major city in Garamas. You and I know, both, Commissar that is not on.'

Duvorac's face registered something like shock; but the voice went on at an even tone. 'Of course, Admiral, such action was very far from my mind. There is an alternative, which would require the utmost skill and exact timing. Garamas has a number of peculiar features. There is a brief period in each day cycle when natural forces cause severe electrical disturbance. Since the power ring was established, this has been intensified. For a period of six or seven minutes between dusk and dark, tracking gear is virtually screened. By careful planning a small ship could be so placed that it could move in to one of the desert areas at that time.'

Varley said, 'It would still have to get out—which is a slower process'—and regretted it as soon as the words were out of his mouth. The answer was obvious and the voice confirmed it.

'But then, Admiral, the defence installations are powered by the ring. Once it is broken, the ship will be in no danger. Except, of course, that it must withdraw without being identified. Otherwise O.G.A. could move on the pretext of protecting Garamas's neutrality. Your Commander Fletcher has been studying the problem and will know where best to make a strike. At his next visit to this headquarters, he can report direct to you on this link.'

'He can do better than that. I'll have him come out here with *Petrel*. This will be the last action before the squadron is

82

relieved. Fix it with the port authority for her to leave. Destination Lados. I'll intercept him as soon as he quits the gravi-sphere.'

'You will choose your own man, of course, Admiral. But if I may suggest it, Fletcher would be ideal for this mission. He is very resourceful.'

Varley looked at the time disk. Conversation, even on the scrambled link, had gone on over-long. Not a doubt that some monitor would have hooked on by now and no code ever devised could not be cracked eventually. He said shortly, 'Thank you Commissar. Over and out.'

Frazer said, 'He could be right. Fletcher might be the one.'

'That's so. But give Duvorac half a chance and he'd run the squadron. I didn't want to give him the satisfaction of thinking I was following his line. But Fletcher will do very well. Order general stations. Lift off in one hour. Move into a parking orbit outside interceptor range. *Petrel* could be out in twelve hours. As soon as she rejoins wheel Fletcher in.'

The people's choice opened his eyes to a dim light and looked up expecting to see the underside of a market stall. Whoever had followed him in had a rare bouquet of exotic perfumes; but taking up where he left off, he grabbed for a hold that would bring the body close in as a protective cushion.

Silky hair covered his face. Small, firm breasts shoved warmly at his chest. Xenia said 'Harree!' with what breath she could salvage for the chore.

Fletcher held on with one arm and cleared his eyes. There was a pink ceiling three metres off. The room was five metres by six with a concertina door directly facing him. Blue wash walls, a small balcony over right with a dressing chest beside it in bright yellow board and his own over-night bag standing beside it. Orientation was rapid, thereafter. He was in his own pad, on his own bed and he was squeezing the pips out of his busy ally.

He released his grip with some caution. There was no knowing how she would take it. He half expected to find a knife in his throat.

For a count of three, she relaxed, letting gravity press her against him, then she moved like quick-silver, so that she was kneeling over him, knees under his arms, back straight, hands lightly on either side of his head.

'Eet is me, Harree. Aren't you glad to see me?'

Seen foreshortened through the slim parallel bars of her arms, her face was startling in its absolute symmetry. Electrum hair swung forward in an elastic cowl. Eyes were grave, serious, evaluating what he was thinking.

Fletcher put his hands over hers and then worked slowly along until he was holding her shoulders. She was the prototype for Olympia, transmuted out of bronze into bird-frail flesh. Insubstantial as a dream figure.

She said, quiet as a shared thought, 'Not so, Harree. You are not seeing me as I am. You are a romanteec. You project onto me something that ees een your head.'

Hands tightened on her shoulders. He bent his arms bringing her down.

She went along with it, moving her knees, until their heads were only centimetres apart. His hand moved under her hair, with nicely judged component orientation and brought her mouth to home on his own. Very warm, very soft, an unexpected planetfall after a long mission in an empty quarter.

Then she had twisted free, whipped two metres off and was saying unsteadily, 'Not so Harree. I theenk not at thees time. You have reservations about me. At the back of your mind, you remembaire the geneteec code of your organization. You would

84

reproach yourself. I do not want that. Eef we are lovers eet weel be when you have no doubt left.'

Fletcher sat up slowly and shook his head from side to side as if to clear away a mist. She was right, but it was no catch to be so easily read. Also the moral line ought to have come from himself. He said, 'You're a strange one, Xenia. But, for record, you're the most beautiful girl I ever saw. Put me in the picture, then. How do I get to be here?'

'Duvorac was worreed about you. He ees a good man, that one. He peecked up the broadcast at hees console and knew you would be een dangaire. He sent me to warn you and gave me an escort to breeng you een. I.G.O. security uneeforms are very like local police. The crowd thought we were arresteeng you.'

It was a shorthand statement for what must have been a very dodgy enterprise.

'Why here? Why come back here?'

'The broadcast ees ovaire. People hardly remembaire what they thought. Though you must be careful to antagonize no-one eet ees more eemportant than ever to see your friend Yola and have her group find these transmeetaires.'

'How has it worked out in the rest of Kristinobyl?'

'No problem. Only thees sector. Three of four squares only were affected. Two Earthmen and a Passalanian were keeled.'

'So. Nationals of I.G.O. planets. That figures. They'll be satisfied with the trial run. One thing. How is it you resisted the suggestion? You might have been moved to stick me with that leetle knife you carry about.'

'For eet to work, there must be a desire een the mind to teenth that way. Thees ees reinforced. Now I am full of loveeng thoughts towards you. Also I understand mind control.'

85

Fletcher stood up and walked circumspectly round the room. Except that his head ached, he was okay. Xenia's last analysis had an edge she would not intend. He had been made critical of himself. That could only mean that there was a self-destructive agent in his own head waiting to be encouraged. It was not his Ego's day.

A calling pinger started up on the table console beside his bed. It was a welcome diversion and brought him back strength nine, as an outgoing force.

He reached the table in two strides and pulled up a small video screen from its slot. It already had a Garamasian face on it as though the owner had been living there in the dark for some time.

Yola said, 'I'm in the lobby. I got your room number from the letting board. Can we come up?'

'We?'

'I have some friends with me. We came separately. As far as I know nobody has been followed.'

'Surely come up.'

Xenia said, 'That was fooleesh of them. Only one should have come. I weell have a car ready. As soon as you are through, we should leave here.'

'Do that. I'll make it brief.'

Hand on the door, she said, 'Remembaire, Harree, eet ees no good unless you have no reservations.'

She was gone before he had time to reply and he remembered too late that he had not even thanked her for bringing up the relief column.

But then, with her fingers in his head, she probably knew.

Yola's group was five strong. Three young Garamasian men and another girl who had one arm strapped up inside her caftan, but was otherwise a carbon copy of Yola herself.

They sat in a half circle and Fletcher, as the focus of ten, unblinking, obsidian eye disks, felt like a corrupt elder betraying youth.

One, introduced as Termeron, was clearly the leader of the cell and was a tougher proposition than Yola had been.

He said, 'What you say makes sense. But we must be cautious. Vida here is a testament to what can happen when we follow your suggestions. We know that changes do not come easily and that a revolution is not made without the shedding of much blood. That, we accept and will take our chance. But what is at the back of your mind? What advantage is there for you in this?'

'For me, personally, nothing. The trial broadcast whipped up the foreign bogy and was against Earthmen. That was only a start. Eventually, when the network is complete, they will dominate all thought on Garamas. Yours included.'

'That is possible. But if Garamasians are calling the tune, it might be a better one to dance to than one played by foreigners —even the Inter Galactic Organisation. We are working for certain liberal reforms; but we are Garamasians, we are not ashamed of our people. Also, we are not war-mongers. We believe that this planet should be neutral and work out its own salvation without reference to I.G.O. or O.G.A.'

The concertina door slid quietly back and Xenia joined the back row, identifying herself as 'Commandaire Fletchaire's asseestant.' When the group reformed, the psychokinetic battery was reinforced by a pair of brilliant green eyes which were faintly mocking.

Fletcher was suddenly irritable, his head still ached and he reckoned he was listening to the peace-in-our-time bit, which had been a dangerous fallacy down the millenia. When you got right down to it, there were certain absolutes, precipitated out from the mental mush as a hard crystal core at the centre of the human mind. Put it at the least common denominator, there was an influence aboard which in certain moments could be recognized as good. The I.G.O. charter of human rights was in tune with it, even if it did not dot all the i's and cross all the t's. O.G.A. was against it; a personification of the evil principle; a latter-day, graceless Lucifer.

He forgot diplomatic caution and began to speak of what he had seen. Level, even tones carrying conviction. He got round to his own part in it—a representative of the countless thousands who had accepted the draft and put in their years of service, policing the galaxy and keeping the sub-human cultures of the Rim, contained in their bleak quarter.

Yola was looking uncomfortable and twice tried to interrupt, but he went right on, 'Never think you would be left alone to work out your own salvation. Garamas is too useful. Your own state police are gentle lambs compared with the crew you will get if O.G.A. takes over. Don't deceive yourselves. All right. I tell you frankly that what I want you to do is in I.G.O. interest. But you are intelligent. You can see the difference. You must know that I.G.O. is only concerned to see a fair system running. Once it is assured of that, it remains only as an adviser and protector.'

Yola finally got in with, 'You are making us ashamed. Of course, we know there are wider problems than our own. But we have worked for a long time to improve conditions here. Garamasians are not evil people, but bad traditions are hard to change. We have friends in all the engineering departments. We can find out where these machines are. Why could we not seize them and use them to propagate the opinions we hold?'

Fletcher thought wearily that he had wasted his time. But Termeron saved the day.

He said slowly, 'As I understand the Earthman, that would

not do. It might succeed. But it would not be right. In the last analysis, means are as important as ends. If we did that, we would be no better than the fascists. Men must be convinced and that is a slow process. Yes, we will work for you. You shall have the location of these transmitters. What then? How will you set about neutralising them? To inform the state police would be no good, they would not have got this far without protection, or at least passive support from men like Pedasun.'

Fletcher was tempted to give the whole story. He was asking them to put themselves in danger for something that might not be necessary, if the ring itself was cut. They deserved the whole truth. He reckoned that the political angle was shot through with cynicism. It was a continuing marvel that any good ever saw the light of day.

But whatever damage was done, the ring would be repaired. It would be easier to seize the stations while they were non-op. He had no brief to go farther. There was some force in the cynical dictum that too great a secret is soon widely known.

They were ready, however, to be convinced and he could say with frank honesty, 'That, I do not know. But you are not betraying your own people. These stations are manned by Laodamians or Scotians. There may also be a hook-up with fascist cells working for a *putsch*. In any event, knowing what the machines can do, you have no choice.'

Last out, Yola hesitated at the door and gave him a long, straight look, Unsmiling and enigmatic, she seemed to have come of age over the last week. Xenia speeding the parting guests, got a special, deliberate stare. Then she was gone, after the others.

Xenia put on a false air of concern, 'What have you been doing weeth that girl, Harree? You are geeving that tender conscience of yours a hard time. She ees jealous of me. Have you been geeving her presents too? You are a Bluebeard. But I must warn you. Eet ees dangerous on Garamas. Eef her father ees a tradeetionaleest he weell make you marree her.'

'Did you get that car?'

'Yes sir. Don't worree, I weell not tell. As you say een your reedeeculous language—I weell keep eet under my bushell.'

'Don't mess about Xenia. Just go on ahead. I'll be right behind you.'

At the door, she dropped the act and said, 'You deed very well weeth them. Eet was very empresseeve. You really beelieve what you say. I hope you do not have any designs on that Yola or I might be tempted to steeck her weeth my useful knife. Be queeck. We should go.'

In the lobby, Garamasians who had been in the area during the broadcast looked more speculative than hostile. They were recalling that there was some reason for dislike, but could not precisely remember what it was. There was enough residual force in the memory to make them suspicious.

Without wanting to top a popularity poll, Fletcher reckoned that the role of public enemy would be one that he could not sustain over a period. It undermined confidence. No wonder minority groups were aggressive. They had to be or end up demoralized and hating themselves.

It was a silent ride, with Xenia deliberately avoiding meeting his eye and leaving half a metre of clear space between them on the squab.

At the I.G.O. penthouse terminal, she said, 'Duvorac weell see us at 1600. I have work to do. See you then.'

Evidence that Duvorac himself had not been idle met him in the ante room of the commissar's suite. It was a large circular room, lit by hexagonal ports in a heavily decorated ceiling. Dominant *motif* was the opulent, baroque buttock, with the total effect that a mixed bag of nymphs, cherubs and satyrs had beaten gravity and were struggling to escape through the roof.

A half circle of bucket chairs round an information console had familiar occupants. Cotgrave, facing, as he came in, fairly leaped to his feet and came across to meet him. 'Commander, glad to see you here. Now maybe we can get a straight story. What goes on?'

They were all there, and the new interest had sharpened them up. In this enviroment, they hardly seemed to be the same men who had been a bad risk in the pen.

For one thing, they were now in full shore rig. White, round-collared uniforms with the I.G.O. blazon and rank flashes in gold pipe. Even Hocker got slowly to his feet, but prudently hung on to a tall green glass that he had just freshened from the bar dispenser.

Bennett as the next senior executive came forward with Cotgrave. 'Any change from that dump can only be good, Commander; but we've been told nothing. An hour ago one of the goons told us to pack, then an I.G.O. shuttle picked us up. Are we to live here in the Consulate?'

Fletcher said, 'It's good to see you out. I'm as much in the dark as anybody. There's a meeting with the commissar at 1600. Maybe we shall hear the score then.'

Hocker said, aggressively, 'And about time, I'm sick to my stomach with hanging about on this beach. Not a piece of tail in sight. Correction. Erase that. Score it out with a sinuous line.' Glass in hand, he was off across the parquet on a course North-East-by-North to where Xenia had appeared between two lotus figured columns in a crotch length apricot tabard and her hair in a shining, tulip cowl.

Fletcher had a momentary flash of intuition. He could see

91

how it would be. They were pulled together for a purpose. This was likely to be his crew. The sooner he got Hocker sorted the better. Without wanting forelock-knuckling peasants in his team, he knew the score as far as discipline went. In a spacer, it had to be automatic. With a five second debate from a crewman, about whether he thought the order was a good idea to himself, a ship could be molecular trash.

Cotgrave said quickly, 'Don't take too much notice of Hocker just now, Commander. He's young and I reckon the waiting has been heavier on him than the rest of us. But he's a good engineer, I can promise you that. Put him to work and he's a different man.'

Everybody seemed to be reading his mind these days, but it was no bad thing to have a co-pilot who could anticipate his reactions.

He said, 'I understand that. The sooner we all get under load the better. 1600 coming up. Now we should know something.'

Slap on cue, a panel glowed over Duvorac's lintel with the legend, 'Commander Fletcher's party enter now.'

Out of the corner of his eye Fletcher could see that Hocker was penning Xenia between her two flanking pillars. Whatever he was saying was taking time. Then she seemed to go along with it and he had a suspicion that she had caught him looking. Whatever it was, she put out a convincing giggle as though privileged to be chatted up by the conversationalist of the decade. Then she prodded the engineer on his sternum with a supple forefinger and drew his attention to the folk migration at his back.

It all looked like a case of instant friendship. Fletcher found himself thinking that he did not like it. Duvorac's first words, however, when they were all seated in a double row facing the plinth, gave him something else to play on his pianola.

'*Petrel* is to rejoin Admiral Varley's squadron. There is a special mission lined up for her and thereafter the tour of duty in this quarter is over. Relief is on the way, and leave which is overdue will be taken in an I.G.O. planet, probably Physcoa.'

Hocker muttered audibly, 'What's wrong with Earth Planet?'

Fletcher turned round in his seat and found the man directly behind him and not a metre distant. Xenia in the next seat watched as if at a NO play. 'Button it up, spaceman. You're here to listen. You'll be asked for your opinion if and when it becomes essential to have it.'

Eyes met for a count of three and Hocker turned deliberately away to look along the row at the rest of the crew. He got no support.

Fletcher let it go. It was going to take time, but he had made his attitude clear.

Duvorac went on, 'It is important that *Petrel* leaves today. I have negotiated the move at a high level, but once it is known, there may be other groups who would put in injunctions for delay. Therefore, I want her out as soon as it can be done. Command of *Petrel* has been given to Commander Fletcher. I have the commissioning authority and sealed orders to give him. Crew will be brought up to strength when she rejoins the squadron. When is the soonest you could lift off Commander?'

'Preliminary checks will take up to an hour; but I believe she is ready to go. After that a sixty minute countdown. Provisionally I would say eighteen hundred hours. Do you agree that, captain?'

Cotgrave said, 'I have not been aboard for over a month. But we finished the minor repairs. She was ready to rejoin on signal at that point. I agree it is possible.'

Duvorac said, 'Very well. I had everybody attend to hear the official appointment. Now I will speak alone to Commander Fletcher for a few minutes. Transport to the launch pad will be along at once. Thank you for your services to I.G.O. and good luck on this enterprise.'

When they were alone, he said, 'There is an additional matter. Perhaps the crew should not know of this. Xenia will accompany you. She is too well known to be of further use in intelligence work on Garamas. Another post has been found. But she could not leave by passenger flight. The squadron will soon be in Physcoa and she can move on from there.'

'There is no hiding place on a corvette. The crew will have to know.'

'She is a sound mathematician. Perhaps you could give her an operational role. Later, she would transfer to *Europa,* where there is special accommodation.'

'Very well. The Scotians have planted a pick-up on the hull. I shall brief the crew and leave it there. What they hear will confirm that it is a simple rejoining operation.'

Xenia, stuck with a non-speaking role sat at the communications desk between Johnson and Ledsham. Anonymous, in the smallest space suit carried in the locker, she was passed over like a lay figure. But she could appreciate Fletcher's problem. The crew had expected Cotgrave to take charge and they resented a new hand on the tiller.

She heard Hocker, by-passing the general net, on a direct link to communications, say to Ledsham, 'We've got a right staff fairy here Tom. For godsake check the data. It may be only a delivery run for that silver crumpet; but he ditched *Terrapin* and nobody yet knows the how and why.'

They did their work. The years of training saw to that. Lift off was a copy-book manoeuvre; but Fletcher could feel that he was not handling a team. In an engagement he would be hard pressed.

Petrel felt right. She was a later marque than *Terrapin*. Handier and more powerful. Potentially a crack unit. Get the human element right and he could take her anywhere at all.

It was a relief to be away from Garamas into a world he knew and could manipulate. Xenia saw the change in him and prolonged her Trappist silence even after the link with the Scotian was broken. When the Squadron came up as a tiny glowing jewel in the zoom lens of the main scanner, she was almost glad to think that there would be a change of company.

Then it began to dawn on her that the rest of the crew shared a serious doubt whether they would make it at all.

Ledsham asked for a report of the Commander's last transmission and even filtered through the intercom, there was a harmonic of simple disbelief. It was echoed in one way or another all round the net and Fletcher said it again with cold clarity.

Swinging in unison with his co-pilot on the tiny command island, he said, 'Hold fast on the auto chain. I'll take her in on manual.'

Xenia working her E.S.P. link in a private bid to know what it was all about, homed in on Ledsham. He was registering a kind of reluctant awe. Course changes involved would mount as much G as a primary blast off and rate split second calculation. The computers could handle it; but a fractional loss of concentration from a human operator and *Petrel* could hurl herself like a bomb into *Europa*'s slab sides.

Now the screen was showing the squadron as discrete units. Five craft, set silver beads on a black velvet display pad,

Europa in the centre with four pencil-slim corvettes outriding in a protective screen.

She tried Fletcher and got a blank. He was utterly committed to the mathematics of navigation, mind working like a machine.

The duty officer in *Europa*'s control room had picked up the tiny speck of the hurrying corvette and locked on tracking computers. Linked on the same net, *Falcon, Drake, Heron* and *Hawk* trained major armaments in concert.

When *Petrel* was a pea-sized globule, she was the focus of destructive power that could disperse her as a faint nimbus of glowing gas. Five computer-based tracking systems monitored the oncoming craft. Coded recognition signals punched out and cleared the air.

McCool on *Europa* took his finger from the general alert button. Then he was looking at an empty screen and by reflex thumbed down the stud, which sent alarm bleeps to every corner of the cruiser.

Varley, first in the command centre, still sealing up, with his visor hinged back, said, 'What is it, Jock?'

'*Petrel* rejoining Admiral.'

'So?'

'Recognition okay; but now she's evaded the tracking gear.'

'You believe she could be hostile?'

Enacted in every command centre of the squadron, there was the same question mark over *Petrel*'s off-beat manoeuvre.

Consequently, there was a full audience to see the corvette warp out of RT, as though by sleight of hand in the single blind vector on *Europa*'s port quarter and take up station with a flamboyant course change, which must have put her crew on the extreme edge of G. tolerance.

Her Commander's level tones coming up on every net said simply, 'I.G.O. corvette *Petrel* reporting for service with Red Squadron. Request instructions.'

Varley, clamping down on a richer text, at the cost of a near cerebral haemorrhage said thickly to *Europa's* captain, for all to hear, 'Get that maniac along to see me, Commander. Stand down, if you please.'

CHAPTER SIX

COLONEL Pedasun, racing for *Petrel*'s pad with a stand-fast order signed by the President no less and still liable to smudge, had to veer off to miss the fireball. Only his rank and visible, simmering temper had gotten him past the check point. Finally, the official had let him through on a reading of the situation, that if he burned himself to a crisp, he would be in no position to sound off and if he did not, he could not grumble either.

The latter angle was however pure speculation and Pedasun proved it false.

Incandescent gas flooded the blast trenches, hot updraughts set his police tender onto its beam ends, his pilot threw everything into a crash climb that pinned the crew to their bucket seats. A fresh air duct channelled a hot waft of sooty debris into the interior, as if *Petrel* had deliberately spat in his eye.

When he finally stepped onto firm ground on the apron in front of the reception block, he was fairly gagging with thwarted rage. Fear past made him vindictive. He stumped into the office, whacking left and right with his cane.

The philosophical official, too slow off the mark to vacate his post for a subordinate, took the brunt of it.

'Why could I not contact the ship?'

'Land lines had been severed ten minutes ago, Colonel.'

'Who was responsible for that?'

'It is normal practice. Part of count-down procedure. The ship makes the break, when her Commander is satisfied that all is well.'

'You agreed.'

'There was no reason to do otherwise, Colonel. Your message came *after* the line was cut.'

'I am not satisfied. You will be interrogated. Take him to my car. Go back to headquarters. Send out my personal shuttle.'

Pedasun spent the ten minutes of his wait, stalking from room to room in the complex spreading *angst*. Daylight wilted and ran symbolically into black night. He laid it on the line that no ship should clear the port without notification being sent in to his office thirty minutes before land communication was cut.

It was a useful security refinement that went some way to pay for his time, but he was still looking for a more solid pay-off when a deferential orderly paged him with the news that his car was ready and waiting.

At the console, he dialled traffic control for a suburban trunk and sat back while the auto pilot took him off. Fifteen minutes later, he crossed a darkened Stymphalus Park on a high lane, then cut the beam and took over on manual.

There was not much farther to go. Five kilometres on, he turned due East, over cultivated farmland now invisible and planed down into the well-lit courtyard of a trim commune, which was the centre of the district.

At this time of day, there was nobody to see him arrive. Farm machinery, parked in rows for the night, filled one side of the square. Most workers had taken the underground mono-rail to their homes in Kristinobyl. Only a handful of mainten-ance staff would be still on the site and those were taking the evening meal break.

A sensitive man would have felt the psychic pressure of the huge empty shell, a caravanserai set in a flat waste; architecturally, a relic of the past, when district centres were fortresses. But Pedasun walked quickly through an open arch and followed a covered way to a corner of the structure marked by a five storey block, solid as a keep.

Easy ramps lit by wall ports worked in an equiangular spiral up the outer wall and he went on to the top.

The last pitch was on the outside and looked out over the darkened countryside to distant clusters of light like asterisks in a lattice. For the first time, he was challenged. A Garamasian, in para-military rig with a carbine hooked on his left shoulder by its strap, stepped out of a shadowy alcove and said 'Garamas for Garamas.'

'Ring of Conquest.'

'The General is expecting you, sir.'

A door in the thickness of the wall slid away and Pedasun went through.

Now he was in a short corridor, brilliantly lit and floored edge to edge with blue thick-piled carpet. At the end it turned through a right angle and widened into a reception area with a desk and a double-leaf door going on.

A young Garamasian woman in a trim black uniform with the interlaced ring symbols of Garamas over her flat diaphragm stood up and flipped a key on an intercom unit. 'Colonel Pedasun is here.'

The reply was inaudible; but no doubt affirmative, because she went on, 'You are to go straight in, sir.'

Inside, the low ceiling crossed by massive open beams made the room appear larger in floor surface than it really was. Twenty metres square, with no supporting piers it gave the illusion of going in every direction like an open field.

Pedasun had a clear walk to the far end where a group of at

least a dozen were in session round a large oval table. Mostly they were Garamasians, but there was one Laodamian and a trio of Scotians sitting together below the salt plugged in to a language cracker. At the head of the board, General Hablon was sitting erect with an A.D.C. on his left and the manager of the complex on his right.

Even folded into a chair Hablon was impressive size-wise. Vertical, he would be all of two and a half metres. A throw-back to the extinct class of war-lord baron that had carved up the Garamasian scene for centuries for mutual profit and entertainment, his round head was massive and expression-less as a marble artifact. Proving that it was not solid through, he made minimal mouth movements and said, 'You are late, Colonel. I have already received reports from the local division.'

Well aware that he who excuses himself also accuses, Peda-sun took an empty seat half way down the near side and inclined his head to the chairman in a composite signal which indicated that he had his reasons and was now ready for any ongoing business there might be.

Hablon took another sideswipe at him by saying to his right hand marker, 'Read back a brief summary. We will all wait until the Colonel is up-to-date on events.

Again Pedasun inclined his head. At this stage, the man was important enough not to cross openly. But he made a private note that in the fullness of time, the security branch would put itself outside the range of the political machine.

Most of it he knew well enough. There had been a set back at the distribution point in Stymphalus Park, but the agency was unknown. In spite of that, more than half the area was covered by a network of transmitters. A test run had been made with success. Supplies could be made good in under twenty-four hours since a Laodamian freighter had checked in with a full load of equipment. In the meantime, there was enough on the ground to do an adequate mind-bending job whenever the call came.

When the man had finished, Pedasun said, 'Thank you. I was, of course aware of all those points. I believe that the fire in the depot was engineered by I.G.O. agents. I was getting close, but they evaded me a few minutes ago by leaving Garamas in an I.G.O. ship. That, gentlemen, is the sort of thing which will not happen when our administration takes office.

'For the rest, there is a civil rights movement among the students and technicians which is gaining some ground in that limited sector. There is no danger. I have informers at the heart of the group. I know that they have been asked to locate our equipment in the Kristinobyl area. False information will be fed to them, When the time is ripe the leaders will be arrested.'

'Why not now?'—Hablon made it sound as though only a fool would have an answer.

'They are well-connected with families sympathetic to the present administration. It is not impossible, but it is not advisable. Later, they will be no problem. We should not complicate the issue at this stage. Selected broadcasts aimed at confusing the liberal position are easy enough. A man who sees too many sides of a question is already defeated.'

Hablon said, 'What have our Scotian allies to say?'

Whatever it was, was unintelligible taken neat. The leading hand of the trio began a staccato rattle of clicks and a speaker on the face of the console delivered it, with a short time lag, in Garamasian. 'We are ready, General, at any time. Both ships are at stand-by alert. Crews can be flown in from the internment centre in shuttles which are held there. Garamas will be welcomed by the Outer Galactic Alliance.'

102

Not everybody looked delighted. Pedasun made a mental note that the commune manager shifted uncomfortably in his seat. Even this small council was a microcosm of the larger society. Many supporters of the movement wanted the liberal administration out without necessarily wanting O.G.A. in. For himself, it was essential. He had no intention of playing second fiddle to a reactionary group led by a military junta. With O.G.A. support, he could go for the top slot, a new man without attachments, who could be trusted. What he did later would be another matter.

As of now, he found a formula to please both sides. 'Your help will be most valuable, Commander and Garamas will be generous. However, we aim, in the first instance, to seize power by popular acclaim. Your task will be to neutralize any attempt by I.G.O. to interfere with our programme.'

Hablon stood up and his round crown was two centimetres from a ceiling beam. He said, 'I will continue my tour of local headquarters. Tomorrow I shall be at the operations room in Velchanos, ready to take overall control. From then on be prepared to act. Garamas for Garamas.'

Except for the Scotians, who maybe took it as too narrow a slogan, he got a full due from the meeting all standing and slapping the right palm smartly to the left shoulder.

'Ring of Conquest!'

On *Petrel*, relief from tension was followed by a resurge of enthusiasm. Xenia picked it up on her psychic crystal and realized what Fletcher had been working at.

Probably only the navigators Bennett, Sluman and the co-pilot himself could appreciate the finer points of the exercise. To the rest it was simply a spectacular manoeuvre, which was a slap in the eye to the establishment. It paid for the long session on the beach. They were in business again as a crack outfit with a man in the top slot who had nothing to learn about handling a ship.

One divergent strand in the symposium, however, she traced to Hocker. He did not put it into overt speech, but the mental field could be listed as hostile. If she could have got him to verbalize it there would have been something like, 'Crazy bastard. Gallery play. Looking for a pat on the head from Blood'n gut Varley. Too bloody clever by half. But you don't fool me.'

Other than that, the calculated risk had paid off. As a new commander, he had aimed to short-circuit the powerful in-group feeling which had built up in the old crew. He had put himself on the same side in a line up against the top brass. Also, if there were any lingering doubts about the *Terrapin* affair, he had made it clear that it was not any failure of nerve or expertize on his part.

Fletcher's own mind was still tightly closed to any E.S.P. probe, except that she judged he was waiting for something else.

When the summons from Varley came, as he had known it would, there was a brief surge of unease. He was not too sure how it would work out at that.

She watched him out into the pressure lock and heard Cotgrave say, 'Good luck, Commander.'

Sealed in the pressure lock, Fletcher reckoned he would need all the luck there was about. He could see his own face reflected on a polished bulkhead, elongated by curvature, a long thin stranger.

Crossing from ship to ship in deep space had never become routine. It underlined dependence on life-support systems. Cosmic loneliness invaded the mind, he became conscious of his hands and the small movements it would take to make a quietus, with body liquids boiling off and tissues exploding apart.

He had to make conscious effort to follow the drill.

He fired a line across to *Europa*'s lock and saw the prehensile grab close on a holdfast. Then he snapped on a toggle from his belt and shoved off.

Outside *Europa*'s lock, he unhooked the thin nylon line and saw it whip back, spring loaded over the backdrop of infinite, violet-black depth. So many multi-coloured sequins of distant light. More worlds than there were grains of sand on Earth's planet. Action or inaction, all was one in this setting. Here was the still centre of the dance, the silence at the core of music, the ultimate confrontation. What could it matter what he did or Varley said?

Xenia's voice spoke quietly inside his head, using Fingalnan which he hardly knew; but the sense was crystal clear, 'It matters to *us*. We are all we have. We are all there is.'

Then he was inside and a yeoman was leading him along familiar trunks to Varley's day cabin.

Concluding what had been a gruelling session, Varley left the psychological vantage point of his executive desk and stumped round to the front.

Changing ground changed his mood and Fletcher knew that he had made out. The tone was still staccato and short on *Charisma*; but it was a point or two down on the acidity scale.

Varley said, 'I'm bound to log you, Commander. There was danger to the squadron, quite apart from the danger to *Petrel*. McCool was ready to blast you. You know that? In his place, you would have done it, no doubt. I see your point, don't think I don't appreciate it. But no more risks with my ships. There'll be action enough to shake your crew down into a combat team. Squadron conference in fifteen minutes. Take a look around and get to know what *Europa*'s control centre has to offer. Call your ship and order a stand down. We may be some time. I'll reserve judgement.'

Round the conference table, set up under an acoustic canopy in *Europa*'s command centre, Fletcher had a mixed reception. Cameron, sitting across, lifted two spatulate thumbs and grinned an unreserved welcome. Grant Crawford, Varley's staff lieutenant, a dark, muscular type looking like an intellectual weight-lifter in his silver grey inner suit, followed the party line and confined his greeting to a non-committal nod. Next to him Colonel Franklin the marine detachment commander and only known to Fletcher by sight, sat stiff as a ramrod and tapped the table in a monotonous, isochronous beat with a silver pencil and looked straight ahead. Cooper and Simpson hardly looked up from their order papers. Anything past was gone for them. Driscoll, heavy shoulders hunched forward and hands stretched out in front of him on the table top said, 'If ever I'm tired of life, I'll get a transfer to your outfit, Fletcher.'

'Do that.'

Dag Fletcher was only half listening. The order paper had his attention. Whatever the higher echelons thought about *Terrapin* and more recently about his unorthodox joining procedures, they had cast him for a very dicey role in the latest exercise.

Varley cut through with, 'You have the detail there, gentlemen. Crawford show us the ground.'

Lights dimmed, a three-sided screen extruded from the deck a metre behind Varley's chair and he swivelled round to look at it. Crawford fed a prepared tape into his console and Garamas appeared three-dimensionally in the alcove.

It was a full relief job and turned slowly on its axis to show every feature. The usual lay-out of land masses was plain to see.

For ease of reference, a latitude-longitude grid and the familiar Earth pattern had been superimposed in a glowing trace, with the meridian running through Kristinobyl.

Seen close, the dark line of the power ring seemed an obvious and feasible development. The land mass, all in tropical latitudes, running between fifteen and twenty degrees north and south of the equator was virtually unbroken except for a single rift valley, sited within twenty kilometres of the one-six-five longitude line. Running due north and south, at right angles to the equator, only mountainous ridges along the coasts held the sea back from running through to make a passage between the two huge oceans.

A seafaring people might have blasted out a navigable channel. But Garamas was land-orientated. Communication across the seas had never been important.

Crawford stopped the spin of the globe and zoomed in on the Grand Canyon. Outer area peeled away as magnification stepped up. The surface of Garamas was unfolding like a flower in time-lapse photography. Here it was utterly dissimilar from the bland downland that surrounded Kristinobyl. It was a harsh world of burning sun and drought.

A running strip showed the build up of environmental factors. Temperature in the outlying areas was knocking sixty degrees Celsius and still rising.

There was no sound from round the table. Every last one had come to planet falls on bizarre and mind-bruising terrain. But this, being set in a habitable planet, seemed unbelievable by contrast with the rest. It was as though all the geological frenzy that convulsed any cooling star, had been concentrated in this one place. Demoniac force had wrenched and twisted the crust, creating huge fault blocks which had tilted and shouldered up in angular fragments. Grit laden winds had ground edges to razor sharp blades.

Colour rioted through the strata. Brilliant blue, veridian, bands of rose madder, streaks and bars of cadmium yellow, all set in the dead black of later basalt formations. Heat eddies distorted the picture, jumbled the lot into an iridescent shimmer.

Crawford was moving along. It was all of a piece. Slice it anywhere and it stood for anti-life. Nobody in their right mind would want to go there.

Even before the viewing eye picked up the spectacular, engineering marvel of the Ring of Garamas, Fletcher had felt the nudge of a sixth sense. This was it. The descent into hell. This was the point of the exercise. Varley had already chosen his ground to do a little sabotage. He was, as Duvorac would have said, hoist with his own petard. He was the one who would be there, on the site, sweating into his visor.

Having conceded that, he was struck, as everyone there present was, by the sheer magnificence of the engineering project which had carried the globe-trotting power circuit across the waste.

The visible surface of the conductor was a white tube on a four metre diameter. Crossing the desert it had run underground and appeared to come from a point ten or twelve metres below the ragged lip of the crevasse. It was supported over the gap on three spidery suspension spans, with two support towers keyed into handy pinnacles that sprang like jagged molars from the distant valley bottom.

There was no surprise that the building of the ring had exhausted Garamas for a generation. This pitch alone was a fantastic national project. Scars on the sand, scattered in a kilometre arc showed the size of the support camp that had once been built to house the labour force. Unless they used salamanders, it would have to have been under heat control for a start.

As they watched, a small platform with a curved under-section that hugged the sides of the white tube came into vision, moving out from below the overhang and Crawford used his last magnification to bring it close.

Even at that, detail was not too clear. But Cooper, who had reached command by way of the engineering sector, said, 'Lubricant. Or painting. Painting I'd guess. Exposed like that, to that heat, it needs round-the-clock maintenance. Probably sprays located inside the hoop. Runs out the other side and back at fixed intervals. That would be too important to leave to robot gear. There'll be a duty crew.'

'Thank you, Commander. That's how I see it.' Varley signalled to Crawford and the picture folded in on itself and disappeared. Visual aids were okay; but Varley had learned from experience that it paid to switch off, when there was speaking to do.

He waited until every eye was on him and went on, 'For reasons which are too detailed to set out, it is essential to make a break in the Garamasian power system. We shall do it there. You will ask why I choose that point.'

Nobody did, but every face showed that it was a good question.

'In the first place it will cause maximum difficulty from a repair point of view. In the second place and most important, it is virtually the only place where it can be done without revealing our identity. That is crucial to the exercise. At all costs and I repeat, all costs, it must not be known that an I.G.O. force is involved. I am outlining the plan to all commanders, though only one ship will go in. The rest will have a support role and must know what is involved.'

Driscoll, a natural for asking the obvious question, said, 'But surely, Admiral, any ship in the gravisphere will be identified before she makes a planetfall.'

'So I believed, Commander. But not so. There is one blind vector. In the brief electrical disturbance which occurs at twilight, tracking gear is jammed. Timing will have to be dead right; but there is an interval long enough for a ship to get in. The squadron will assist by laying decoy flares over the opposite hemisphere. Detail has to be worked out and I want you to think about it and bring up any suggestion that you have.'

Varley activated the screen for himself and brought up the picture again. 'Broadly speaking, this is the plan. Our ship will go in farther along the rift. There is a place where the bottom is clear for a hectare. About a hundred kilometres nearer the north coast. That means she will not be seen from the bridge post. She will come down on the floor of the canyon. Observe radio silence. Show no light. A cutting-out party will use the scout car and fly along the gorge, to reach the bridge area before daylight. There, they will wait until midday. At that time a relief maintenance crew arrives for a twenty four hour duty period. Then they will seize the post, blow the cable at the middle section and return by the quickest route to the ship. Blast off will be timed again to the mid-dusk period.'

He switched off and there was a digestive silence.

Cameron broke it, for once deadly serious, 'It's a bonny scheme, Admiral. No reason against it working out. But once the cable goes, there'll be a fine scurry to that site. They'll work along either way to take a look. They'll surely find the ship.'

Frazer answered him, 'There'll not be as much rush as you might think. Only special craft can land in that area. I'd say

110

thirty minutes before the nearest maintenance unit is ready to leave. That's located south-west in Velchanos, over a thousand kilometres distant. Our ship will have pulled out before they arrive.'

There was only the sixty thousand dollar question hanging about and Fletcher reckoned he knew the answer. He was the least surprised round the table when Varley said, 'It only remains to detail the corvette. *Petrel* will go in. Being a short mission, I do not propose to increase the technical crew. Berths will be filled by a military detachment. Five commandos with sabotage experience and an officer, I leave that detail to Colonel Franklin.

Petrel was suddenly full of supercargo. Fletcher left it to Cotgrave to settle them in. On a forty-eight hour mission there was no problem about permanent quarters, they would get what sleep there would be in the acceleration couches, at battle stations.

Each section had its lay figure cocooned in steely grey, hung about with small arms and miscellaneous gear like so many tinkers' mules.

Their top hand, Abe Carrick, a small burly type, rounded out like a Michelin tyre man with Lieutenant's flashes on his gauntlets said, 'Forget about us, Commander, we're used to waiting. Just get on with the driving bit and give us a cook-house call every so often.'

It was a nice touch of confidence and Fletcher reckoned it could easily be misplaced.

He had a full hook-up with *Europa*'s computers and could draw on advice from some of the best navigators in the business; but the problem was the most complex he had ever faced. He had to hit a tennis court at the bottom of a gorge without a proving orbit to line himself up and with the penalty for a near miss being total loss of his ship. Fractional misjudgement would impale *Petrel* on any one of a collection of needle sharp spars that stuck out from the tortured rock in random disarray.

That would mean not only another ship written off, but the whole safari blown sky high. Literally so. Varley had been explicit on that point. 'One last thing, Fletcher. If you can't get out, at the right time, that is six hours after the ring is cut, blow the ship. Complete destruction. Not a square centimetre for identification.'

'Personnel?'

'What do you think? Where would you go without a ship? *Total* destruction. I'm sorry; but that's the way it has to be.'

The Squadron was strung out in line astern, led by *Hawk,* in so far as direction had meaning in the vacant interstellar places. *Petrel* trailed fifty kilometres back, with its navigators running a final check on calculations which allowed no margin for error.

When he was set, Dag Fletcher called Varley on a personal hook up.

'Ready to go Admiral. Request permission to detach.'

'Granted, Commander. Remember, you're on your own. We can't pull you out if anything goes wrong. Officially I should know nothing about it.'

'I understand.'

'Good luck, I'm sure I've got the right man.'

'Thank you, Admiral.'

Petrel arrowed off like a pointer in an animated diagram.

Command settled like a shroud over Fletcher. It was once again totally up to him, without any filter or intervening agency. Every part of the ship was present as a blue print in

112

his head. It was his habit, when his mind was off load, to run through the modules from the fire turret below the cone to the freight bay above the tripod jacks, ticking off personnel, estimating readiness. He had gotten it to a fine art with *Terrapin,* seeing the ship down to the fine grain finish of the wardroom table.

With *Petrel,* it was more difficult; but he worked along to his own cabin with fair success. There, however, he stuck—with a considerable question mark hanging over the area and enough emotional overtone to have him grabbing for the intercom.

In all the orderly turmoil of coming and going and settling the final details of the assault, nobody had mentioned Xenia.

Unless Crawford or some other had whipped her out unknown to him, she was still there, sitting on her trim, silvery can in exemplary patience.

The command cabin was overfull for private chat and seemed suddenly even more crowded when her voice came back with bell-like clarity to the inside of his visor, 'Harree, I'm tired of looking at these leetle star maps on your roof. When are you coming to your bed?'

Fletcher slammed a run of figures through his computer. Course changes, times for a trip across to *Europa.* New start. It was not on. As it was, he needed every minute to be in the right vector. There was no tolerance left. She would have to stay, It was something else to notch up Varley's blood pressure.

Cotgrave was looking his question, as one fish to another in neighbouring tanks. There was, anyway, no possible chance of concealing even a small stowaway on a fully manned corvette.

Fletcher switched direct to his co-pilot, 'We still have our spy. She was not transferred to *Europa.*'

Reaction was immediate and one more proof that Cotgrave had identified with him in a team situation, 'My fault, Commander. I should have fixed that. I got involved settling in the marines. Not to worry. It's only another forty-eight hours for her. She can serve the coffee in the wardroom. Make a change for all hands.'

'I'm glad you think so. Stand down for one hour. Minimum movement about the ship. I'll go and tell her the score.'

On the way, he visited every module from the subsidiary command post below the power pack, to the small gunnery control in the turret where Carrick had made his quarters. It was necessary, but he wondered how much of it was a simple delaying tactic to keep away from his cabin.

Finally he knew she had to be faced and when he slid back the hatch, he reckoned he had been wasting his time.

There was a non-military smell of some exotic powder that she had used inside her suit which was lying over a chair ready for instant use. She was busy at the small wall mirror dramatising her eye make up, wearing brief triangular pants in lime green as a big gesture to the rough military life. But although as feminine as a girl could well get there was not an atom of sex tension in the dielectric.

It was a mission and there was work to do. Even when she turned to greet him and looked pleased to see him, there was no erotic overtone about. 'There you are, at last. Don't blame yourself. I wanted to come and I deeleeberately kept out of the way. I have a feeling here—' this time a delicate finger tapped her forehead—'that you weel need me on thees affair. We work together like your Charley and Joan.'

'That's as maybe. But right now, if you want to help you can get dressed and go along to the wardroom. Like that you'd disturb the crew's concentration.'

'I know *that*. Evereebodee eesn't *cold* and *eenteelectual* like you Harree. You'll see, I weell be a beeg help. A shield for your backside.'

Petrel was dropping like a silent stone. Fletcher was a machine, an extension of the electronic gear that had lined them up unerringly on the selected target. His voice was metallic as any robot's as he reeled off the last instructions, holding back retro until the dark lips of the gorge were filling the main scanner.

When Engels fired his motors with a reflex that cut every record for the move, the set was bathed in a brilliant orange that brought up detail in a lurid spotlight on a neglected corner of hell.

Petrel checked, in a surge of deceleration that tried to pluck every man out of his foam couch. It was against all belief that the fabric of the ship could take it. Then the hydraulic jacks touched down for a full due and she was trying and failing to bounce herself out again.

Red lights flickered across the screen and a raucous hooter began to sound. Grey coolant streamed past the vision ports and blanked the scanner.

Cotgrave said, 'Damage report.'

Bennett said, 'Freight bay. Pierced by a spar. Collision bulk-head closed.'

Petrel steadied, flexed slowly to full height with a screech of tortured metal that vibrated through every module, and was still. It was over. They were down. Whether they would ever lift off again was another matter.

Fletcher said, 'Thank you, all hands. Secure the ship. Repair party outside. Mr. Bennett break out the patrol car.'

Heat gauges depressed by the coolant started to climb again.

115

Hocker, recording for the log, was looking at them in open disgust, he said, 'Christ. Only look at that. Sixty-nine Celsius and still going up. We'll fry out there.'

CHAPTER SEVEN

DAWN, on the desert side of Garamas, was not held back by any landscape feature. It flooded in a quick-moving. yellow-ochre tide over flat reaches of dung-hued gravel from a circular horizon.

Six men, close packed in *Petrel*'s scout car, watched its progress on the miniature scanner, until it lipped the gorge and declared itself as if a light had been switched on in the plexiglass dome.

Half a kilometre ahead, the flyover for the cable was out of direct vision round a twist.

Bennett, in the pilot slot, had brought them down on a slab that angled out twenty metres below the jagged edge and Fletcher reckoned that with the shifting iridescent colours of the slab top as a back cloth the microgrooving on the hull would be camouflage enough, unless some asbestos mountaineer actually tried to tap in a *piton*.

There was not likely to be one. External heat gauges were in the red quadrant at seventy Celsius and the indicator for extra-vehicular activity was reading a maximum of fifteen minutes.

Abe Carrick, hunched phlegmatically in his gear, stirred himself to say, 'You'll have to take us nearer Commander. If there's a blockhouse, we could be ten minutes getting inside. That leaves ten minutes to work along the cliff. Not on.'

That was not the only reason it had to be quick. Any local commander finding himself under attack would send out a report to Kristinobyl with a description of the attacking party. Pictures even. Although I.G.O. flashes had been taped over, there would be no difficulty in identifying the gear as point-of-origin Earth planet.

Fletcher said, 'Timing has to be right. They'll expect the relief. It's the only chance of getting inside without sending up an alarm. We'll take a look at the ground. Then we'll get some rest. Mr. Carrick with me. Mr. Bennett take charge here. Radio silence. Minimum movement.'

There was no atmosphere lock on the small car and a gust of furnace heat beat in as the hatch went back. Out on the slab, they could feel the heat of the rock even through the thick, insulating foam pads of their inner soles.

Carrick reached the cliff face and worked along the slab looking up at the overhang. Half a metre from the edge, he found what he wanted and stood fast, feet, astride, swinging a grapnel.

It went up sure and true into a custom-built V and he leaned his weight on the line until the tines bit and held. Then he slewed round his harness until the power pack on his back was at his chest. He fed the rope to the take-off spindle and thumbed down the switch. Fending off with his feet, he appeared to walk up the wall.

There was a pause at the top, as he checked the desert for movement, then the line snaked down and Fletcher hooked himself on.

When they were both standing on the edge, Fletcher checked his time disk. Four minutes out of their fifteen. Also, at midday it would be hotter and suit limits might fall to twelve or less.

They went on in silence, two apocalyptic figures, moving

118

in a surrealist waste land. Seen close, there was more evidence that a large settlement had once been built in the area. Mounds and tumbled stones, marks of foundation trenches; it added another dimension to the desolation.

Five minutes covered a direct line from their point of entry to where the cable should be, crossing the oblong promontory which jutted into the gorge and hid the car and the block-house.

For the last twenty metres, they went along on hands and knees, zig-zagging between low banks of cover, in case any roving periscope should make a periodic sweep of the outback.

At the edge, there was a change in texture that spelt out the deliberate work of man. Smooth ashlar, fine stone that had been imported to the site, capped the edge for four metres.

They were directly above the cable.

Seeing it from the ground, the carrying structure was huge, an engineering marvel for any place in the galaxy. Here it bludgeoned the mind.

They lay flat, heads over the cornice, suit gear working at overload to clear sweat that ran down their faces like a wet mask.

Fletcher took another look at his time disk. Ten minutes on the nose. Already past time to head back.

A vibration from below, communicated through the stone and all the insulating layers and he held on to see what was to come.

It was the maintenance trolley. Straddling the cable and running on rail guides set in the superstructure, it trundled out from its housing in the cliff face.

Tubular half-hoops began to spray fine jets that shrouded the cable in white, glistening mist as it moved along.

Fletcher gauged distance to the nearest pillar support feature and began to count. At that rate it would reach the centre span in five minutes. Twenty for the whole operation.

It was a statistic to carry away and work on.

He crawled to the right hand edge of the paved arear and looked over. A steep ramp, ribbed with footholds had been cut into the rock and led down to the level of the cable. That was the way in. But it could only be taken slowly. If there were viewing ports on that side, nobody could reach the entry hatch, without setting himself up as a plumb target.

Carrick was tapping his visor, holding his wrist up and pointing to his time disk in a clear mime.

Fletcher nodded and they started back.

Alone, he knew he would not have made it. The spectacle of the man-made bridge crossing the gorge would have held him against himself. As it was, he carried the picture like a glowing eidetic image in his mind's eye. As hominoid, he had to be proud of a species that could build like that. It was an enduring triumph for *homo sapiens,* who had taken and tamed a totally hostile piece of his environment. It forced a reappraisal of the Garamasians. Whatever aspects of the social scene were out of key with his own way of life, here was vision and courage and achievement that nobody could fault.

It went against the grain to be the one who had to destroy it. Even if it was likely to be done at the cost of his own life. Worse than that, he had put in the boot himself, giving the idea to Duvorac. He had left the whole crew mobilized to repair *Petrel,* but God knew what damage they would find when they eased the rock splinter out of her hull.

Both problems were going in a wheeling cycle in his head and he checked his heat gauge. After its long session in the red quadrant, the needle had swung definitively to NON OP. There was only the time it would take for the fabric to warm through by simple conduction.

Carrick lowered him down the cleft on a friction drag and

followed on a double line. With the whole set in a red haze seen through streaming sweat and a clouded visor Fletcher orientated on the shuttle and forced his body to move. Half way up the slab he stopped, hit by a new idea. He could veer off, walk over the edge, duck the choice and end all such confrontations once and for ever. He could imagine himself floating down into oblivion. The bridge would remain. Or at least some other hand than his own would destroy it. He stood still, moving his head left and right, heat filling his eyes and his brain and his chest in a suffocating cloud.

Xenia's voice, speaking from inside his head, like a commentary from a burning bush, moved him forward. She was standing in his head, a small, silver figurine arms stretched out in welcome, holding, of all thing a bronze, lighted Aladdin's lamp in her left hand. He tried to reach her and she remained the same distance away. She was saying something that he could not quite catch and he said, 'What is it? Say again?'

Bennet said, 'Easy, Commander, easy. It's okay. You're home and dry.'

Fletcher said thickly, 'Where's Carrick?'

Answering for himself, Carrick said, 'Here Commander. I guess I was lucky, my suit kept operational right to the door, but the air conditioner's a write-off. Now we know for a fact what the tolerance is. We have five hours to dead line. Take a spell before we work something out.'

Xenia, concentrating to project herself at a distance, judged she had let Hocker get too close. She had heard the hatch slide away and home again and knew who had come into the cabin; but she had remained stone still, orientated to face towards the distant car, hands outstretched.

121

Other than the fact that her hands were empty, she was as Fletcher had seen her, a taut, silvery nude, who could have modelled for Blake at the centre of a sunburst.

After three sessions with the repair gang, psychic phenomena were lost on Hocker. He had a shrewd idea that the mission had struck a terminal phase and was all set to gather what flowers of today were within reach.

Hot breath was riffling the hair on her nape and his hands had homed on her shoulders before she moved.

Space crew reaction times had to be fast, but Hocker was left with his hands sawing foolishly on air. Then she was back, this time with a slender knife lunged like a fencer's foil at his Adam's apple.

There was nothing to mistake either in the blazing green eyes. Nothing could make Xenia look ugly; but it was the expression on her face rather than the needle prick of the point that sent him back until his shoulders fetched up against the hatch.

There was only marginal satisfaction to be had in what she said, fairly spitting it out, so that he could feel the air on his face, 'Your commandaire ees een trouble. I try to help heem. Eef he dies I weell keell you for a sure theeng. Get out. Tell the captain, I am coming to see heem.'

With the hatch between them, Hocker felt the reaction. He was a fool to be so easy. He had moved automatically down the companion and stopped dead, debating whether or not to go back. She had gotten the upper hand by surprise, Knowing what to expect, he could watch out for that knife. Give the tramp a thorough going over. It would add to the pleasure that she was Fletcher's apple.

He hesitated, held between stimuli like Pavlov's dog. He unbuckled the heavy equipment belt from his inner suit and weighed it judiciously. A tannoy overhead solved his dilemma.

Cotgrave's voice said, 'All hands assemble in the Command cabin.'

When he reached it, taking his time, there was a full house. Cotgrave swinging slowly on the command island turned to watch him in and said with unusual sarcasm. That's nice, Dave. I'm glad you could see your way to join us. Maybe your brilliant engineer's mind will throw light on our problem.'

Thick-skinned though he was, Hocker recognized that silence was the better part. But it gave him another chip to carry. He edged round to the power desk and took his own seat, next to Engels. He felt no better when Xenia followed in. She had shrugged on a set of white overalls turned up at wrists and ankles and picked her way through the press to Fletcher's vacant seat as though by right.

Cotgrave said, 'You've all had a stint working outside and you know the damage. I believe we can't do the repair that has to be done in time for lift off at eighteen hundred. With radio silence on, I can't reach Commander Fletcher. Once he blows the cable, the balloon will go up. I want your judgement. We have nine hours. I want us all to know what we're up against. Power One?'

Engels shifted uneasily in the spotlight. He was still in his space gear with the visor hinged back. He had just come in and it was his report that had moved Cotgrave to take time off for a conference.

'There's a two-metre tear in the freight bay. That, you'll all have seen. The spar came in and went out again at an angle through the outer skin. If it had come straight up, I guess we wouldn't be here arguing the toss. Replacing the floor of the bay is straightforward. We can do that. But the side panel's seriously weakened. It's a stressed job. It held up as we came up; but it bears major load at blast-off. I couldn't guarantee that we'd take her up. That side could open like a tin can and rip right along. It ought to come out. Splice in a fresh rib.'

'Can you do it?'

'Sure I can do it. But it takes time. A base depot would want twenty four hours.'

'What would you want?'

'Nothing less. Maybe more—when I have the section out and get a clear look at it.'

Cotgrave said, 'Fair enough. I'll endorse that. Communications. What's the score for you?'

Johnson exchanged glances with Ledsham and got a brief nod. They were two of a kind. Taciturn to the point of being surly, in spite of their professional trade as communicators. There was even a good deal of physical similarity, both being short and dark with neat sideburns, though Johnson, senior by fifteen years had a vivid patch of white hair over his left temple. He said 'No problem, Captain. Some gear down there is shot. But nothing vital. As soon as the new panel's in, we can wire up what we need in thirty minutes.'

Being a navigator himself, Cotgrave had left that section to the last. He knew basically what Sluman would have to say, but he asked, anyway, for the record.

Number two in the section, Sluman had not previously spoken for navigation in a conference. Next to Hocker, he was the youngest crewman, thin and lanky with a long face and a wedge of brown hair falling over his forhead. He shifted it with his left hand, cleared his throat and started too loud, so that his voice fairly echoed round the cabin.

'No damage to the trim, Captain. I'd have to weigh up when the new material's in place. There'd be a correction to be fed in to the computer. Ideally there should be a flight trial. An error of point one of one per cent could take her into the cliff. But I guess we could do it.'

Cotgrave pivotted slowly on his chair and looked at them

all. He knew the dead line and suspected that Fletcher had fall-back orders. He even had a suspicion of what they were. But as far as he was concerned, he had to go ahead as though this was a routine repair job. He said, 'There it is, then. We all know what we have to do. Next team out in five minutes. Get as much rest as you can, when you come in. By the time, the Commander gets back, I want the damaged section stripped out ready for rebuilding. Okay?'

As the crew filed out he met Xenia's eye and the doubt at the back of his mind turned to certainty.

When they were alone, she put a warm hand on his arm and said, 'Nevairetheless, Captain, you are right. We must go on as eef eet ees *posseeble.*'

Early in his office, at penthouse level in the security tower, Pedasun spent time at a long observation window, looking out over Kristinobyl.

In some sense, it was more his city than the government's.

In his mind's eye, he could see the strands of his power going out like invisible lines of force to every precinct. He was well placed to make a killing. Once the situation was fluid, his own organization would be the only one to remain intact, on a nationwide basis. All his main subordinates were hand picked. There would be no fifth column to watch.

Nevertheless, he was not wholly at ease. There was something that did not add up about the sudden withdrawal of the I.G.O. corvette. Duvorac was no fool. He did nothing without a reason.

But the political balance was too delicate for direct intervention. There was no getting round that key proposition.

He flipped the side of his thigh with his stick. Whatever the old green frog got up to, would be too late.

He gravitated to his personal console, a wall-to-wall job, with an inset map of Garamas glowing on the three metre screen. Pat on cue, a call sign bleeped from the tannoy and a waiting signal—the interlaced rings of Garamas with military insignia as an overlay—filled the scanner. He said, 'Ring of Conquest' and knew that the distant receptor would identify his voice and clear the channel.

There was no picture and he needed none. Hablon's voice was unmistakable.

'I am at Velchanos. All groups are ready. What is the situation there?'

'There are enough transmitters in place to cover the area. Every major city has its network. In one hour we shall begin broadcasts. This time there will be riots all over the city. We shall be in a position to make arrests where we like under cover of restoring public order. By this time tomorrow, the government will be completely discredited. Then we can spread the idea that only martial law can keep the peace. You will be ready to fly in with your staff and the units you have already contacted.'

'That is very good. I shall not forget your co-operation. Keep in touch on the hour. Garamas for Garamas.'

'Ring of Conquest.'

It was as well that there were no pictures. Even with the long start on dead-pan ambience, given by the Garamasian face, Hablon might have been uneasy.

When the screen blanked, Perasun was saying softly to himself, 'Co-operation. You say co-operation. You dumb ox, you wouldn't set out a box of toy soldiers without help. I'll co-operate until you do your job. Then watch out Hablon. I'll give you three weeks.'

Still sitting at the desk, he took a small silver key from a fob pocket. Below the presentation tray, a deep oblong drawer pushed itself out and a video on a square cradle came up from the cavity.

This time, he traded pictures and his own miniature screen glowed with an image that few would want in a cameo. It was the Scotian who had been spokesman at Hablon's local conference. Pedasun named his name as though he knew it well. 'Commander Toron. I have issued passes for your crews. They will be taken out to your ships in security cars. You know what to do.'

Toron's mouth moved and the translator trailed by two seconds in giving the text. 'I understand, Colonel. We have had enough waiting. *Idmon* will remain in the port. I myself will take *Alope* out and maintain a parking orbit above Kristinobyl. No I.G.O. craft will land without your approval.'

'Good. This is a personal arrangement. Take orders only from me. It may be that others will try to move you out of station. But only my direct voice on this frequency is official. O.G.A. recognize me as the negotiator for Garamas.'

'That is understood.'

Pedasun cleared the link and selected another. This time the face on the screen was Laodamian, a farouche job with a low, sloping forehead that might have belonged to a space ape, except for the eyes—which were large and full of intelligence. He said 'Full coverage. As of now. Put out the programmes in sequence; but repeat the anti-I.G.O. loop every other one. Except in the Polytech area. There, I want them brought out on the streets in a mob.'

The Laodamian grinned showing a fine set of canines. He looked as though he had been given a meaty bone.

When the screen was clear, Pedasun looked at it in silence. That was another thing. He had no liking for his allies. What they could do for *him,* they could do for somebody else. As soon as he was set, he would have them out of it. It was no accident that the revolution's watchword was 'Garamas for Garamas.' It embodied a deep-seated element in the national character. In spite of the years of operating a neutral *entrepot,* they would prefer to be left alone with their own destiny.

He spent the next hour leafing through the detail of the *Putsch.* Reports began to filter in. He had said that he would not take any outside calls and monitored a conversation between Duvorac and his own control room in which the commissar was trying to establish who had given permission for a Scotian frigate to blast off.

It was early for chief officials to be at their desks in Government House. No doubt Duvorac had tried there first and found no answer. That was not surprising. Whoever was there would be equally baffled by it.

At 1138 hours the first call that meant personal involvement came in. The precinct security headquarters, which took care of the polytech area, reported that thousands of students had left the campus and were assembling on a public square.

He rang through to his adjutant, 'Four riot cars, a hundred specials. I want every man in standard riot gear dressed as government police. Flashes covered. Wait for me at the porch.'

This was something he would enjoy. Liberals were a disease in the body politic. This time, he would have them where nobody could protect them. Those that were left, when their riotous assembly had been put down.

Inside the Polytech it had started slowly. When the first transmissions of subliminal suggestion started up there were not many students about. Those that had arrived early at culture's coal face were the dedicated researchers who had a problem to solve and had settled in at study alcoves to hear the word from selected tapes.

Minds on load were not so easily infiltrated. But the persistent message worked its way in at every partial loss of concentration.

Yola, who had time to make up, found herself taking a second run through a small jewel on factor analysis and put it down to too many extra-curricular activities. She found herself thinking about the Earthman Fletcher. How far was he to be trusted?

Even in the matter of bringing a gift, he had shown how little he understood the Garamasian customs. By accepting it, she had virtually agreed to a pairing proposal. If he could be so insensitive in that area, what reason was there to expect that anything he did could come from a real knowledge of Garamasian needs? Fear the Greeks bearing gifts was an ancient warning from his own planet's collection of wise saws. And that would include any importation from an alien culture. It was time to speak up for Garamas.

She shook her head and restarted the tape. 'The mathematical analysis of the factors determining performance in a series of operations can be approached by . . .' God, even the preamble was making no kind of sense. They ought to be out in the streets, people acting rather than people thinking. She stubbed the pause button. Restlessness was growing so that she could not sit still. Without any clear idea of where she would go, she stood up and walked quickly out of the booth.

Others had done the same. Small groups formed and drifted aimlessly out into the circulation spaces.

A muted pinger on high C started up to signal the first lectures of the day; but there was no move to enter the theatres. Newcomers were not entering the tower blocks at all and those already inside went out to meet them.

All over the campus instant demagogues had set themselves up on any handy feature and were addressing packed meetings.

Yola recognized Termeron standing on the centre plinth of a fountain, hair glistening with spray, holding on with one hand and making lavish gestures with the other. As she pushed near enough to hear what he was saying, there was a loud yell of assent from the auditorium.

If she had been free to evaluate it, she would have heard the hysteria in it. But no longer a free agent, she responded as though to a logical proof. Whatever he had said was right.

Even when she got within earshot and listened to a polemic, knocking every principle she had ever held, she went along with it with shining eyes. It was a revelation. It was their duty to give the *hoi polloi* a lead. The present liberal government had been and was a disaster. Only a reversion to traditional Garamasian values would give the planet its soul back. Out with all the foreign devils. Garamas for Garamas.

The Laodamian broadcaster allowed some time for the ideas to ferment, using subtle reinforcement that seemed to be supplied from within the group itself. Then he began to feed in the new thought of a move into the streets.

When the moment came, there were five thousand students packed in the open spaces between the towers and they flowed out into the approach trunk fifteen abreast, arms linked, stamping in rhythm, shouting every third step 'Garamas for Garamas.'

Yola went along in the middle of the crowd, carried along physically and mentally by the mass. As the leading files debouched into Crotopus Square there was a momentary slackening of tension as if the close, containing pressure had come off.

The Laodamian manipulator was watching the scene, judging whether the demo had enough head of steam to be self energizing and had cut his transmission to an empty carrier wave merely giving general stimulation.

Recall sounded a warning, she knew what had happened . . . They had all been tricked. Even those who knew about the mind-bending transmitters. Unless that was all an invention of Fletcher's. Could it be that he had given them that handout to make them disbelieve what their own minds told them was best for Garamas?

But that was too clever, even for an Earthman. She saw Termeron up ahead and began to fight her way towards him. Maybe between them they could sort it out. In any case, he should be warned.

Youngsters on the edge of the crowd had begun pulling up paving tiles and were pitching them through the lower windows of the tower blocks that bounded the square. Noise was notching up into a frenetic clamour.

Twenty metres off, she saw Termeron through a random gap in the mob that now seemed to be slowly gyrating round its centre. Before it closed and she was forced further away, she saw his face—pale, serious, troubled. He knew. She began shouting, 'Stop. Listen'. Beating around at every handy chest with clenched fists like a Raggedy-Ann doll gone beserk. But it was one thin, etiolated strand in a growing cataract of random din, that was finally drowned out by the howl that went up when four government shuttles dived in from every quarter, spraying a fine green mist of choking gas, to clear themselves a space to land.

Watching for the right second, the Laodamian boosted his prepared anti-government slogans so that the troops, spilling out of the cars with oblong shields up to their brows met a blind charge that surged over those who were crawling about the *tesserae* with streaming eyes.

Still holding on to a sagging intuition that there was something rotten in the state, Yola registered that every last one of the new arrivals was wearing shiny ear cuffs below the white domed crash helmets. It was the final and irrevocable proof. They carried personal screening against whatever was in the air.

Another thought struck and stopped her dead in her tracks, oblivious of the surge of movement that left her isolated except for certain still figures who were totally out of programme. Whoever had sent in the marines, knew all about it. Not the government itself then, or they could have attacked the broadcasts at source. It was a complex, double manoeuvre, more sinister than a plain issue of keeping public order.

She was still trying to work it out when two specials appeared on either side and grabbed her arms. No solution had come up when she was pitched to the floor of a shuttle and the door slammed at her back.

Petrel's scout car hovered like a dragonfly under the rim of the ravine a hundred metres from the blockhouse.

Outcrops of multi-hued spars screened them from its slab side; but Fletcher had banked heavily on the heat factor. Insulation would be vital for long-term occupation. There would be no point in making observation ports on a side which was unassailable. Working in fifty metre stints he had crept along the cliff face with long stops wherever there was room to put down the skids.

Now he was watching the scanner which gave them a half-moon picture of the apron above the post. Anytime now the relief shuttle should be coming in.

Heat had stabilized at seventy-three Celsius, with hotter gusts rising from the bottom of the pit where angled mirror surfaces made pockets of thermal agitation.

Half the car's power pack was committed to fighting a rearguard. They were out on a technological limb with no fall back. Even the phlegmatic Carrick was getting edgy and tapping the buckle of his harness with a horny thumb.

When it came, action transformed the set. From an empty quarter where only a fool would choose to be, they were part of an inhabited land as though the grey shuttle which whipped onto the screen and touched down on the ashlar strip was connected to Velchanos by a glowing streamer.

It was still flexing on its skids as Fletcher said 'Now.'

Bennett cut refrigeration and gunned for a crash climb. The car bucked out of the gorge as if booted in the belly by a gigantic toe.

Fletcher had the firing grip of the laser tube that ran the whole length of the car's axis and shut his mind to the sure knowledge that what he had to do was an act of war, which, if it was less than a hundred per cent successful, could embroil the galaxy. He said, 'Right along the spine,' and they went down like a mosquito homing on a succulent flank.

CHAPTER EIGHT

BELATEDLY two guards spilled from the Garamasian transport, both in clumsy refrigeration gear like a collection of articulated boxes.

It was a pantomime sequence as they clumped around in slow motion trying to sort out who was doing them wrong. Then one saw the car and ponderously lifted a machine carbine that sent up a lazy line of tracer.

Hammer blows crossed the underbelly of the car in a single lucky strike, then the laser was breaking up the shuttle. It appeared to fold in on itself, before it opened like a vermilion flower edged in black smoke.

A small plosive thud hit the car and lifted it ten metres with Bennett fighting for control. When he brought them round for a second run, it was all over, smouldering debris was scattered for a hundred metres and the two guards had disappeared.

Carrick said, 'Blown over the top, by god.'

Face set, Fletcher said, 'That's a pity. We could have used those suits. Now we have to do it the hard way.'

Bennett had them down in a neat landing, a metre from the rim and they baled out into furnace heat.

Phase one was Carrick's and he led his three marines, Adams, Curtiss and Powell for the edge of the paved strip at a shambling trot. They went down on one knee in unison, a grotesque chorus line and used vibrators to slice out holdfasts. Then they hooked in claw grabs and slithered backwards over the drop.

Fletcher, pulling against the tension of the car's spring-loaded hoist line leaned out with his heels chocked on the rim and had a bird's eye view of the action. The four marines hit the surface of the ramp fifteen metres below, checked for two seconds to cast off and draw bulbous blasters, and slipped out of sight under the overhang in a classic reversal of the Indian rope trick.

Fletcher signalled for down and Bennett lowered away. As his feet came clear of the wall, nervous reaction cramped his diaphragm. The whole scene could have been watched from inside the blockhouse. Even now, very now, Carrick and the others could be charred cadavers and the marksman was drawing a bead on his descending crotch. He was a fool to think they could do it this way. A cosmic blunderer, whose anonymous hand was destined to set the Galaxy ablaze.

A heavy body brushed against his dangling legs and for a nonasecond he believed it was a shot striking home. But it was Adams, Carrick's Number Two on the stick, on a search ploy that became plain as soon as he could see.

The ramp ran down for another five metres and stopped dead at a blank wall.

Insulation had been the over-riding factor even here. Not only was there no observation port, there was no visible entrance.

Fletcher unhooked his toggle and went forward to where Carrick was running gauntlet hands over the smooth stone face. Already the suits were fighting a rearguard against heat. Sweat running into his eyes, Fletcher plugged a wandering lead into Carrick's chest console and hissed 'There has to be a way in. Some kind of recessed lever.'

135

'Adams is checking the slope for that thing.'

Behind this wall, they could be talking to Velchanos, drumming up a support column. Passing on pictures that would identify *Petrel*'s car. He could be too late.

Carrick stumbled on it, banging the toe of a clumsy boot on a six centimetre stub almost flush with the rock face where the blockhouse melded into the side of the gorge. He knelt down on all fours to get the full view in direct vision through his visor. Then he squatted back on his heels like a hound dog.

Fletcher mimed urgently for him to shove it over and they lined up facing the blank, grey wall, blasters trained waist high.

When the opening appeared, Fletcher was not immediately aware of it. By instinct, he had expected it to be in the centre, but it was far left, against the wall of the cliff, a low, narrow slit strictly for one-at-a-time entry, a blue painted culvert into the thickness of the insulation.

Carrick, nearest the site, was moving before the opening was fully made. His bulky figure plugged the gap from edge to edge. A defender could not miss.

Dag Fletcher was working out how they would proceed. Fire cover and movement. Drag the body clear. Work on until somebody succeeded in getting to the centre. Anyone could do the job. They had discussed it in fine detail in the hours of waiting. Nevertheless there was no hesitation when he shoved Adams aside and ducked into the tunnel.

Almost at once, there was a bonus in heat loss. He could feel the sweat cool on his face as the recirculating gear dried it out. Up ahead, Carrick was plodding forward, until he disappeared round a right angle turn.

There was the impression of a cool spacious chamber, as though deep in a natural cave. Through a long horizontal slit

136

of window, glazed in great depth, there was a magnified panoramic view of the gorge and the first features of the flyover.

Carrick had thrown every atom of muscular drive into a sprint that had taken him to the centre of the room and was sawing around for a target. Fletcher was out with his back to the near wall followed by Adams and Curtiss. Powell having stopped back to close the hatch was ten seconds late and found them set up as a tableau to spell out surprise, surprise.

The place was empty.

Carrick checked the air and found it good. Suit gauges had plummetted to twenty Celsius. He tipped back his visor and stuck up both thumbs in confirmation.

Adams revealed as a bullet-headed youngster with a thin scar down his left cheek said, 'What's the angle, chief? I thought there was supposed to be goons in here.'

Carrick said, 'Don't be disappointed, Rod. There'll be other ways of breaking your fool neck. I reckon intelligence got it all wrong. Not for the first time. There's a daily inspection visit. Some myopic agent put it down to a personnel switch. But what the hell. It's fully automated. All it needs is a pat on the can at the right time which does nothing but good.'

Over by the computer spread which filled the rear wall edge-to-edge, Fletcher thought it was a little hard that he should have drawn a Vaudeville duo in life's lottery and broke it up with a call for action.

He said, 'All right. So it's a bonus. Powell, up top and bring down a half dozen limpets. All hands search around for a hatch to get below. Every once in a while that paint *howdah* will have to be given a manual check out. And Powell, tell Bennett to bring the car onto the ramp. He can clear away your securing lines while he's waiting.'

In the event, he found the floor opening himself in a fast, totally concentrated survey of the control panels. Instructions

137

were in Garamasian, but pictograph insets gave a lead to the main functions. He spun a wheel rheostat and a section of floor began to dip.

Adams, who was currently crawling over it on hands and knees, looking for a tell tale crack in the parquet, scored high on reaction time by grabbing for a solid edge and holding on.

Carrick said, 'You found it Rod. Good, good, keep it marked,' and ignored the long string of profanity that came from the hanging man.

A fresh smell of paint welled up from the hole and a courtesy light, that must have gone on as the floor opened, revealed a long workshop with the paint sprayer itself standing ready on parallel rails.

Adams looked down and dropped a metre to the deck, standing between the hoops. He called up. 'Neat. Very neat. Two linear motors to shift it along, paint pumped to the hoops from a reservoir. Should be one in every home. Outer wall swings back to let it out. Don't for godsake monkey with any switchgear till I get out of here.'

Carrick said, 'What I like to see is a keen man. Just button up, Rod and we'll give you a run out. When it stops, get on the parapet and excavate a site for the limpets. You'll be breaking new ground.'

Adams looked up without any pleasure at the four faces poked over the well head. He said, 'You look a right lot of zombies up there. I reckon I'm safer by myself.'

He sealed up and lay flat on the support lattice which linked the outside of the hoops, with Fletcher at the console and conscious that he was already two minutes past his midday deadline.

The floor rose and locked. A vibration underfoot marked the ponderous shift of the outer door. Powell, at the window called out, 'there he goes. The White Rajah, by god.' Once clear of

138

the exit, Adams had shifted round to sit crosslegged on the top of his excursion module. All he lacked was an elephant gun.

Shut down of the paint spray function might exist, but the control eluded Fletcher. He could and did accelerate the linear motors to a top speed of twenty kilometres in the hour, which whipped Adams to the centre span in under three minutes, but atomised paint, driven with tremendous penetrative force curtained the moving hoops in a white mist.

Adams's suit had turned from silver grey to a dazzling white carapace and they saw hs movements were slowed up when the platform stopped and he climbed out on to the carrying structure of the cable itself.

Minutes dragged by. Even Carrick said, 'The crazy bastard. He'll run it too fine. Burn himself to a crisp. He must be trying to shear through it by hand.'

Then the distant figure raised a white arm and swung back onto the paint sprayer.

Fletcher whipped him back and Carrick was fairly hopping with impatience to get below and dropped as soon as the gap was big enough to squeeze through.

Adams had not moved. Reflex action had kept his grip, but he was unconscious.

Fletcher had dropped after Carrick and went straight to the supply racks. Drums of paint and, at the end, what he knew must be provided for periodic flushings of the gear, carboys of clear solvent with a mechanical pump and spray. He sluiced down the snowman and Adams slid free off the hoops, turning steel grey under the stream.

Carrick had his visor back and was slapping his cheeks, 'Come on Rod, snap out of it. You can sleep in your bed.'

Eyes opened one at a time, focused briefly and closed again. Adams said, 'Why didn't we bring that Fingalnan *bint* along to play nurse. It's all set. You can have it.'

Powell had found and activated a telescopic duralumin ladder and Adams climbed into the control room. Curtiss handed down six, blue-black hemisphere limpets and Carrick hung them round his belt. He said formally, 'All set, Commander, make it as fast as you like.'

Up above, a calling bleep sounded out and Curtiss said urgently, 'Call from Velchanos, chief. I guess that patrol should signal when they arrive. Somebody getting anxious.'

Fletcher spun the rheostat and the floor closed. Now he was familiar with the gear and Carrick fairly shot into vision like an electric hare.

With the insistent nag of the call as a background, the time seemed longer; but the chronometer denied it. When they saw him signal for in, he had chopped two minutes off Adams' time.

When they washed him off the cradle and got his dome off, he was still hot to the touch and spent a half minute breathing the cool air as if it was spiced with all the perfumes of Arabia. Finally he asked thickly, 'Will somebody tell me how the goons built it? I don't reckon anybody can work out there for more than five minutes. They'll never repair it and that's a fact.'

It was fair comment. Last out of the control room, Fletcher looked round the orderly installation and felt like a homicide. This was the summit of technical development for this planet and a major achievement for men anywhere in the Galaxy. He was setting back the clock and no one knew how it would turn out.

There was no comfort in telling himself that he was a man under orders and that he was on the side of the righteous.

What was right? Only conditioning over the years had given him one set of attitudes. A different environment would have given him another.

In the end, there was only yourself and a feeling for the

truth, which ran like a carrier wave underneath all the snatches of argument. There was a purpose abroad that could be recognized, in moments of insight, as stemming from a source which was good. I.G.O. was tuned in to it more or less. Unless he was deluded into self-grandeur he had to accept that. He was not the only moral man in the universe.

They were all waiting in the car and he said, 'Take her to a hundred metres. Be ready to ride out the blast.'

It was ten minutes after the meridian when he said, 'Hold it there,' and switched in the beam that would detonate the limpets.

After ten seconds, Bennett, reading his mind, said hurriedly, 'It's going out, Commander. Full power. Every relay must be hammered.'

Fletcher said, 'Keep trying Number One,' and set himself to analyse the operation from the beginning.

He had primed the limpets himself. They had to be right. In any case every one of six could not have developed a fault. There was some factor he had overlooked. Not heat. He hefted a spare from the rack and looked at it. Marked for use up to two hundred Celsius. It was hot out there, but not so hot.

Then he was looking at the stub lever which was brought through to the outside of the case for exceptional use by a mechanical trip wire. Carrick would have given that clearance to move when the relay tripped and released the trigger.

He saw Carrick in his mind's eye raising a white arm to be run back. That was it. Paint. Paint had run down the case and gummed up the release. Anybody trying to shift it would go up with the cable. There was no way of defusing the bomb once the relay had tripped.

They were all looking at him and he followed the old military precept of giving an order when in doubt, any order being better than none. He said, 'Back to the ramp, Number One.

There are more ways of killing a pig than drowning it in cream.'

Inside the blockhouse, the call signal had stopped and Fletcher had silence for his manoeuvres. It made the weight of attention more difficult to bear. They were all looking at him as though he was following a prearranged plan and nobody wanted to be rated as stupid for asking what it was.

It came to him fully formed as he dropped into the paint bay and it could have been a personal pay-off for humility and putting confidence in the system.

He said, as though he had gone there to do that thing, 'Drain the paint tanks. Fill up with solvent. I reckon the triggers have stuck. We'll run the trolley out and park it over the centrespan. As it empties, it should wash the casing clear.'

It was only when he had the *howdah* in place and was lumbering out through the tunnel, that he recognized there was no time limit on this fuse. It could blow as he reached the door and take them into the gorge before the car could lift away.

The same thought was in Bennett's mind and he was gunning for a crash climb with Adams and Carrick still heaving Fletcher over the coaming of the hatch.

The car crawled for height like a crab, listing to port with half its human load in a struggling mass against the bulkhead.

They had the hatch closed and Fletcher hurled himself into his bucket seat. Now he could see between his knees through the observation panel in the deck. The trolley was still in place and under the concentrated flow of solvent, the cable was showing black as layers of white paint washed away.

He found himself willing it to happen, visualizing the mechanism of the limpets as if he could break the last resisting thread by psychokinetic force alone.

When it happened, his mind came off load as though it had

suffered a parallel rupture in its circuitry and for a count of three he saw only a flare of brilliant, multicoloured light. Then even through the car's acoustic shell and the protective gear he heard a high-pitched scream rising and cutting out as it passed beyond audio frequency.

Eyes focusing again and bracing himself, as the car rocked in a force nine gale with dust and small trash hammering at its hull, he saw every dial on the console going in a crazy spin.

Carrick, breaking radio silence, was broadcasting on his external speaker in a crackle of static. 'Holy cow. Only look at that.'

For a hundred metres from the point of fracture, the huge tube, glowing with an intense cobalt nimbus, had peeled free from its supporting viaduct.

On the near side, freak force had thrown the broken end down and an eye-aching arc was spitting into the floor of the gorge, turning the impact site into instant lava. The far end reared up, an immense brilliant elephant trunk, finding an uneasy balance, the phallic symbol of all time.

Not much of the viaduct structure had been breached. Ten maybe fifteen metres. Repair was feasible, but it would occupy national resources for some time to come. It was just the way Varley had wanted it.

Fletcher saw it as a wound in the ring of solidarity forged by professional men. He felt like a murderer, who would now give anything to staunch the flow of blood and have the victim say something however banal.

Military usage bridged the gap. Bennett had finally pulled the car into level flight and went by the book. 'Heading North North East by North. Manual navigation only, Commander.'

Fletcher said, heavily, 'Check. Hold that. Follow ground features. Quick as you like back to *Petrel*.'

143

In Kristinobyl and every other major city on Garamas, rioting crowds stopped in their tracks. Men looked stupidly at each other and at the improvised weapons in their hands.

Respect for authority and above all respect for property was built in from way back. As the Laodamian carrier wave collapsed, they were left with their basic attitudes uncovered by the ebbing emotional tide.

Groups on the perimeter of the dense crowds began to peel away, anxious to get back to a home base and think it through.

They were met by a new wave of malcontents, mainly women, who had stuck to the hearth and skillet.

Total power failure hit like an act of god. It had not happened in living memory. A keening wail rose from every dormitory area.

Duvorac, depending for his life on auxiliary systems, keyed in an emergency supply, which was held ready, and looked sourly at his time disk. Twenty-five minutes behind schedule. That argued more difficulty than Fletcher had expected. Time for identification. This desperate piece of surgery could be fatal to the patient.

He set himself to wait. Nothing more could be done, until it was clear which way the government and the people would jump.

Pedasun in his eyrie, stared at his blanked screens in disbelief. A degaussing feature in the security tower block had kept out the subliminal broadcasts and he had no personal monitor to tell him they had stopped.

Technicians gave him a limited emergency power feed after five minutes of frenetic effort, which drove him to the edge of frenzy. When a reduced service gave him one picture of

Kristinobyl's main square, dispersal was already well-advanced. There was a litter of broken paving sticks lying everywhichway, a swirl of broad paper streamers. The popular insurrection had gone out like a damp squib.

A harassed official at the Power Centre gave him the score. 'Major breakdown in the Ring circuit, Colonel. Unprecedented. Located in the desert area. Probably at the crossing of the Great Gorge. No estimate can be given for the repair. Maintenance crews are leaving Velchanos now.'

It was too pat on cue. A coincidence too big to swallow. I.G.O. must have engineered it.

He moved to his long window and tapped the sill with his cane in a monotonous rhythm. Somewhere there was a gain to be made from every situation. If he could pin this on to I.G.O. as an act of sabotage, there would be no need for subliminal suggestion. The ring was a symbol to every Garamasian. They would unite against any faction that struck at it. With Hablon ready to bring in his regiments they had lost nothing. In fact this could be a final proof of government ineptitude. They could not even guarantee the safety of the main prop of the economy.

Many levels below the penthouse, Yola sprawled on her back on the tiled floor of the brig, saw the single light go out and then reappear in complementary colour on the ceiling.

Intellectually, she knew it was all illusion, but it was evidence of a kind one part of her physical equipment was still working at normal pitch.

The same was only marginally true over the whole field. Even pain had passed its perihelion and was reduced to a dull brutal ache.

A small amber emergency light came on over the door and she screamed by reflex as though she was still on the table in the interrogation room.

It had been short, but concentrated, a preliminary softening up session, so that next time she knew she could hold nothing back. The specialist staff had handled them half a dozen at a time, stripping them and pegging them out with electrodes taped to every nerve centre, and she could still hear her own screams amongst the others in a crescendo of pain.

This was the cue-in for the next phase. She began to tremble uncontrollably and felt her bare skin begin to crawl, triggered by its own logic.

The same thought had hit Termeron. He was struggling to sit up, shoving away a fellow nude who was lying across his legs like any cadaver in a death pit.

She forced herself to move one balled fist pushed against her mouth in a heroic bid to plug back any sound.

They met at the door under the amber light. Termeron shoved feebly against the panel and felt it move. Then they were looking along a dimly lit white-tiled corridor, which they could not remember having seen on the downward trip.

He said, and his voice sounded infinitely distant from his own ears, 'Power failure. Field too weak to hold the wards. Must get out, before they fix it. Get the others.'

Some were already sitting up. Given a task, Yola found she could move. She was even able to think in terms of a viable future and, on that level, she was acting like the only *houri* in a fraternity bath house. But libido was too low for lechery. For the majority, she was an abstract pair of hands trying to usher in a present that they did not want to know.

Finally, she had a round dozen on their feet and moving like zombies to join Termeron in the corridor.

He called in, 'Leave them, Yola. There's no time. Let's go.'

At the end of the corridor, the line shuffled to a halt before

146

the closed trellis of an elevator trunk and Yola said bitterly, 'It's no good. They don't need guards down here. We can't get out.'

Termeron shoved the grille and it slid clear. The large service cage had sunk down to mechanical stops, a metre below floor level and there was a dark, narrow gap just above head height.

Setting his teeth, he reached up and drew himself painfully over the lintel. Then he reached down to help Yola.

When they were standing on the roof of the cage, in a draughty funnel with a ripe bouquet of must and axle grease, she could see a distant point of light like looking up a tall chimney.

Termeron was checking manually round the walls of the shaft and said, 'It's all right. We can do it. There's a line of holdfasts. Tell them to hurry it along and follow me. Don't look down. Just keep looking up at me.'

It was some way from all right, on any reasonable count; but she was feeling better all the time. There was hope in the air, struggling for a toehold in the murk. Maybe they would get out. She passed on the message, modestly leaving out the last bit, which would probably occur to the climber upward, anyway.

Bennett circled *Petrel* twice, before he brought the car into its hanger. The heat of its outer skin triggered a decontamination sequence and a cloud of heavy grey coolant shut them down in their capsule. They could have been anywhere or nowhere.

Fletcher saw the stripped-out freight bay projected in his mind's eye with a question mark in Tempo Inline. He checked his time disk. Fourteen hundred on the nose. Blast off at eighteen hundred. A repair crew in a base workshop would never do it in the time.

Another thought evaded the censor and floated up for conscious evaluation. It took a positive effort to beat it back, and the chore of doing it gave it more precise definition and a form of words. 'This is no more than justice. You are a homicide. What you have just done represents the loss of untold millions of man hours. You are a barbarian, family tree going back to Attilla. The only partial absolution you have is to lose your own life.'

He threw the book at it, a man under orders. The end was justification enough. As the car clicked onto its cradle and the gas was sucked clear, he had it licked and a new voice was speaking, so loud that he looked round for Xenia. It was long range welcome, however, beamed on her one-to-one psychokinetic link. 'I'm glad you decided that, Harree. I wanted to help you, but you'd always have held eet against me lataire on. You can only do what seems to be right at the time. Come and talk to me. I'm veree lonelee.'

For all the point there was in getting the score from Cotgrave, he might just as well do that thing. But since he had the rule book out, he might as well follow it to the letter. He shrugged out of his suit and climbed down the main trunk to where Cotgrave and Engels were methodically building the replacement bulkhead.

Cotgrave straightened wearily round face grey with strain, 'Sorry Commander. Not a hope in hell of meeting your deadline.'

'How long?'

'Alf says another twelve hours. The crew have gone flat out. But they're tiring. It's wholly hot outside. Can't do more than a six minute stint. Once we get the bulkhead back, refrigeration solves that, but there's a lot of circuitry to refit. How did your mission go?'

'Wholly hot, as you say. Completed. We can expect visitors anytime at all.'

'Shall I carry on?'

'Do that. And pass the word to all hands that they've done well. One other thing.'—Fletcher paused and looked out through a direct vision port into the grotesque confusion of the gorge. It was no time to tell men who had sweated their guts out that they had wasted their time.

'Commander?'

'Drop everything at eighteen hundred. Every man to report to the control cabin.'

'Full gear?'

Again Fletcher paused. They might as well go out in full regalia, a working unit, striking a hazard. 'Full gear.'

He stopped off at the command cabin and found Ledsham doing a duty stint at the main scanner.

'Nothing moves, Commander. But there's bad screening. I only get fifty kilometres without the probe.'

'Hold fast on that. It would be seen by more than it would see. As soon as anything crosses into range sound General Stations. *Anything* at all.'

'Check, Commander.'

He moved slowly towards his cabin. Fifty kilometres. The very fastest atmosphere craft on Garamas would take four minutes to cover that. There was time to get to the command island from any part of the ship, and pull the plug that would bring the walls of the gorge in on *Petrel* and bury her atomised fabric in an instant crater.

Or should he do it now and be sure? No pilot could fail to identify an Earth rocket ship. Whatever gain there was to be in the enterprise could be lost by a count of seconds.

149

Xenia met him at the hatch, as he slid it away; hair brushed down straight in an elastic cowl that rested silkily on her shoulders. With a rare flair for improvization, she had turned a piece of fine steel chain into costume jewellery and having no costume had snapped it on at skin level.

It slanted across her hips with the free end dangling down the right thigh emphasising that pose which had occupied sculptors through the millenia; a pleasing swing of the hip, weight taken on the right foot, left leg bent as if to move. She did not in fact move and Fletcher had to stop or knock her down.

The hatch slid closed behind him; but he was looking into vivid, green eyes, that were not making any effort to seek out motive or probe into his own thoughts. She knew what was scheduled for eighteen hundred and was leaving the action to him.

It was a blank cheque to be filled out for any sum.

She did not move, except to tilt her head back when her breasts were nudging pneumatically against his coveralls. Then her hands travelled up his arms and linked at the back of his neck.

Sophistry told him that with dissolution coming up on the clock, the rule book could hardly apply. Then he faced it honestly. Rule book or not, it was a moment out of a lifetime which stood on its own logic.

Very gently, he put a hand on either side of her head under the warm bell of hair.

She said, 'Harree,' neither as a question nor as answer, but as a statement of faith.

CHAPTER NINE

FOR centuries, Power Control in Kristinobyl had kept an emergency plan on file. From time to time, it had been taken out and dusted off. Even, on rare occasions, a keen, new administrator had tried out a dummy run. But over the years, solid efficiency of the ring system had come to seem like an immutable law of nature. It was inconceivable that its power could be withdrawn.

Consequently, Pedasun had some difficulty in getting anybody to tell him a plain tale.

He was as guilty as the next man of putting his faith in the public service and found that the security communications net on emergency power could only guarantee a reach of fifty kilometres round Kristinobyl itself.

Troubles, following precedent, did not come singly. A sweating guard mounted the long spiral staircase to the penthouse to tell him that some of his key internees had made a jailbreak and had taken a security shuttle from the pound.

The messenger had been drawn by lot and expected a vindictive counterstrike. He was agreeably surprised, therefore, when his chief did no more than slash the back of an office chair and ask a question on a different tack.

'Is there a long distance car on the pad?'

Relief was so great that he hardly understood and was

151

within a touch of getting the cane across the face.

'Do you hear, you fool? Is there a long-distance car?'

'Oh. Yes. Yes, Excellency.'

'Have it fuelled. Six men and a pilot. Stand by as of now.'

'Certainly, Excellency.'

'Get on with it, then. Move.'

Pedasun walked twice round his room and the exercise seemed to clear his head. Coincidence was out by a sea league. The break had been deliberate. He grabbed up the video and put it down without making a call.

No good. The prisoners still below would have no knowledge of it. No Garamasian would have done it. Certainly not a Government faction. That would be psychologically impossible. They lived by the power of the ring, its technology was their life's blood.

Scotians could do it. They would need no motive and could not be trusted to see long-term interest against the present pleasure of devastation. But they were thin on the ground. All accounted for. No. It had to be I.G.O. The strategy of it would fit well enough. Set Garamas a local problem. Reduce her main asset of abundant cheap power to make her less attractive as an O.G.A. base. Even without knowledge of the right wing *coup*.

Where did that put himself? Not so differently. They had miscalculated. The only loser would be the liberal government. They would figure in the public mind as too feeble to maintain order. The average man would turn to Hablon's party. National pride would look for a scapegoat and also want to see a political leader who could repair the damage.

Hablon should come in now and take over at the height of the confusion. It was a message that nobody else could take. He would go himself and be seen from the beginning as one of the leaders of the movement.

But first there was a local piece of business. He picked up the video once more and called the I.G.O. Consulate with a personal request for Commissar Duvorac.

There was some satisfaction in seeing the Venusian under strain. Duvorac's emergency power supply was not as flexible as the city main and his elaborate life maintenance systems had been thrown out of kilter. Eyes half-closed, face grey as ash, he said wheezily, 'What can I do for you, Colonel?'

In so far as he appeared to be moving well in that direction, there was no advantage in saying 'Drop dead'—so Pedasun got to the point. 'You have already done a great deal. This sabotage of the ring will not advance your cause. Be sure the people of Garamas will be told whom they have to thank. By breaking the non-intervention status of a consulate, you have torn up any claim to diplomatic immunity. You may or may not know it, but I have a military ship positioned above Kristinobyl. It will depend on your actions whether or not a selective strike is made on the I.G.O. complex. We have every right to take retributive action.'

If he expected Duvorac's heavy face to mirror guilt, he was disappointed. There was no visible change, as the Venusian said, 'You assume too much. Before you do anything so foolish, think what you would say to the task force that would surely bring you to account. Do not think either that O.G.A. would be easy partners. They want Garamas for their purposes, not yours.'

'How does that differ from I.G.O.?'

'To a man who does not see the difference, explanations would be useless. What else do you have to say?'

'Only this. Until you have clearance from me, all I.G.O. personnel are confined to the perimeter of your complex. No signals outside Garamas are permitted. Breach of either of these orders will be regarded as a hostile act.'

'How long is this veto to operate?'

'In the first instance for one week. Then it will be reviewed.'

'Has the President been informed of this?'

'Commissar, let us not be naïve. Before the week is out there will be a new government and that government will negotiate with you.'

Pedasun picked up his peaked cap and stick, fished in a closet behind his desk and came out with a heavy service belt that held a blaster and a pouch of fuel clips.

When he was ready to go, he called in his adjutant and spent ten minutes on detailed instructions for the on going scene in Kristinobyl. He finished with, 'I am going to Velchanos Accept no orders from anyone except me, or General Hablon in person. Is that understood?'

'Certainly, Excellency.'

'Garamas for Garamas.'

'Ring of Conquest.'

First in *Petrel*'s command cabin, Dag Fletcher took his seat on the command island and looked bleakly round the familiar set. Many ships, many actions and they had all brought him to this point in time. The sky had been good for flying.

Xenia, anonymous in a bulky suit, clipped herself in at the communications desk, but used E.S.P. to speak directly into his head. 'What weell you tell them, Harree?'

Physical contact had finally put him on her wave length and he could say through the same medium, 'The truth.'

'There ees truth between us.'

'Yes. Of a different kind.'

'There ees only one kind of truth.'

Cotgrave came in, followed by Engels. Hocker, Ledsham and Johnson came in as a group. Bennett and Sluman were the last of the crew. A week ago, he had not known they existed, now they were people looking out at the world from an individual point of view as he did himself.

The marines settled in and Carrick called through from his post on the first step, 'All set Commander. Listening.'

It was seventeen fifty-five. Fletcher flipped on the log for the last record he would make and needed no one to tell him it was a waste of time.

But it was usage. And only usage would get him through what he had to do. Run it as a standard count down with oblivion as the pay-off.

He said harshly on the general net, 'Commander to all hands. I don't have to tell you the state of the ship. You've done everything a crew could do, to put her in operational trim; but we can't make the deadline. Ordinarily, I'd take a chance, there's the slimmest possible hope that we'd clear the gorge, before she began to break up. But this isn't an ordinary mission. More hinges on this than you know. There's no margin for error.'

Fletcher shifted the small command island in a slow sweep, so that he faced every executive desk in turn.

'If we miss the scheduled time, we cannot avoid being seen by some searching craft. If we wreck *Petrel* the effect is the same, she will be identified. I don't have to tell you what the Garamasian government would make of that. Or what O.G.A. would make of it. It must never be known that an I.G.O. military craft carried out this act of sabotage. Orders are clear and inescapable. I am charged to disintegrate the ship.'

There was no sound on the net. The command cabin had gone still. Each man in his capsule digested the edict according to his nature.

Having lived with it for twenty-four hours, Fletcher recognized he had an unfair advantage. On the other hand, it was a daily condition of service. Every mission was an act of faith in a million components that could fail at any time. Every planetfall was a bonus and a flouting of all statistical probability.

Cotgrave said, 'How long have we got?'

'No time, I'll run it as a countdown from eighteen hundred.'

'Some personnel could get clear.'

'In fifteen minutes, the heat would get them. Then identification would follow. Not possible, Captain.'

Hocker began to swear in a monotonous stream as though he did not realize that he was speaking aloud.

Cotgrave said sharply, 'Hold fast on that Power Two. Has anyone any useful contribution to make?'

Fletcher said evenly, 'Thank you. I record formally that all hands have carried out their duty in exemplary fashion. Count down as of now.'

He selected a small key from the array on his console and shoved it over. A panel slid clear in the desk top and a set of micro switchgear extruded itself on a springloaded platform.

The controls duplicated in miniature the standard items already in view. Operation was parallel, but using this set, the reactor was overfed and turned itself into a runaway pile.

As the sweep second hand of the chronometer above the main scanner homed on eighteen hundred, he pushed in the activator. Muted bleeps on orchestral A sounded out every fifth second.

Hocker, overloud, so that his voice vibrated round every visor asked, bitterly, 'How do you pin a gong on ectoplasm;

Fletched emptied his mind. All the fragments of present time had imploded into this one. And there was no use to be made of it. Only to endure, without movement, for the short time it would be. Stillness to merge into stillness. It was not heroic. It was not anything.

156

Xenia was there with him, another silent, accepting mind, moulded from an alien substance, but basically the same. All conscious life had the same qualities. That was a truth he was late arriving at and could not be filed for future reference.

A voice on the net was irritating him. Why couldn't they take it in silence?

Ledsham was saying urgently, 'Commander, I have a message. Very faint. I.G.O. call sign. From Kristinobyl. Calling *Petrel*.'

For a nonasecond, he wanted to ignore it Another count of five and the procedure would be over the top and irreversible. But habit died hard. While it was still in one piece, his ship had to answer on the command link. He moved deliberately and broke the auto chain.

When it was done, he found he was sweating with relief and had to steady his voice before he could speak.

'Print out.'

Every head turned to the main scanner and Ledsham presented the text as a running strip, a caption to a still picture of the darkening desert.

'I.G.O. corvette *Petrel*. Suspend action. Await new orders. Acknowledge.'

'I.G.O. corvette *Petrel*. Suspend action. Await new orders. Acknowledge.'

It was starting its third repeat before the full meaning had gone home. Fletcher said, 'Answer that, Communications One. Brief as you can. Tell them we're standing by.'

On the general net, he said, 'There may still be a use for *Petrel*. But she must be ready to go. Captain Cotgrave, all hands on the repair detail.'

Fletcher received the call three hours later. Suspended in

hot darkness above the tripod jacks and nudging a new cladding plate, a centimetre at a time, towards its niche, he found Xenia projected in his head like a pearlescent statuette and was inclined to be irritated.

Her voice, not using the communications net got as far as 'Harree,' before he snapped back, 'Not now, Xenia. Save it.'

'There's a long message. Ledsham has eet een the decoder.'

Ledsham's voice took over on the mechanical link, 'Commander, instructions from I.G.O. consulate.'

'Hold it. I'll come aboard.'

Printed out on an official blank, it was Duvorac's swan song. 'No further transmission is possible. Screens are being sited round the I.G.O. complex. Government has collapsed. Military Junta known to be ready at Velchanos. Leaders will leave there at first light to bring military forces into Kristinobyl. Use *Petrel* to search out H.Q. and present I.G.O. veto, without delay. Threaten instant destruction. Believed to be sited in farm commune at 039716. Scotian frigate *Alope* in parking orbit over Kristinobyl. Ongoing action at your discretion. I.G.O. authority vested in you. Good luck. Out.'

Ledsham said, 'It was very faint, Commander. Local jamming on. But that's the text.'

Thinking aloud, Fletcher said, 'It's not on. We can't move her before dawn. Not even then, the way things are going. We've handed it to them on a plate.'

Visor hinged back, face grey with strain, Cotgrave hauled himself through the hatch and stood leaning against the bulkhead. Xenia looked from one to the other, seemingly out of programme.

It was up to him at every level and he was tired of making decisions. Now Duvorac had given him *carte blanche*. The signal he was holding cleared him of all previous commitments. *Petrel* would not be ready in time. He could hang on, repair her, then blast off to hell out of it. Rejoin the squadron and report the situation. Varley might belly-ache; but he could not go beyond the Commissar's writ. If that was the action which seemed to him best, he was entitled to take it. The situation on Garamas had developed differently from what had been expected. O.G.A. were in, it could not matter whether *Petrel* was identified or not.

But it did matter. It would matter to him for the rest of his life. There had to be something he could do.

How long in the car to Velchanos? Seven hours, pulling out all the stops? Make it just before dawn. Delay them, one way or another, until *Petrel* could be brought up with armament that could devastate a province?

Xenia had been keeping out of his head and beamed in with the equivalent of hand clapping and timbrel beating. 'That's eet, Harree. I was begeening to theenk I deed not know you at all. I weell come. I know thees place. We weell throw an ultomato een their works.'

Aloud Fletcher said, 'That should make anybody think twice. I'll take Carrick, Hocker, one marine—Adams. Travelling light we might just do it.'

Cotgrave said, 'Sorry, Commander, have I missed something? What have you in mind?'

'Break out the car. I'm going to Velchanos. Bring *Petrel* along as soon as she can move. Low trajectory, there's a Scotian up over Kristinobyl. Drop on this reference. If I'm not there, take off and rejoin the squadron. Those are your orders.'

Xenia on the E.S.P. link was fighting for feminists everywhere. 'You are aiming to leave me behind. You cannot do that. I am not a domesteec cow to be left in the laager weeth the non-combatants. I have thees feeling. You weel *need* me on thees enterprise. Beside, I can guide you. Eet ees too eemportant for personal judgements. I promeese I weel not eenterfere.'

'I know Scotians.'

'Eef I am not afraid for *myself,* eet ees no business of yours. You do not love me, to use your reedeeculous Earthy expressions.'

Fletcher said, wearily, 'I guess your weight makes no difference. Okay, come along. Keep your mouth shut and your hat on and they'll reckon I've brought the cabin boy.'

Ledsham looked from one to the other and like Cotgrave believed he had missed a link. It was a crazy mission at that. Philosophically, he turned to his desk and continued with a horizon sweep. It was a comfortable routine. While he was doing that, he couldn't be expected to be doing anything else.

True to her resolve to meld with the furniture Xenia packed herself in the small freight bay at the back of the column.

Fletcher took the pilot slot with Carrick beside him. Adams and Hocker sat in the rumble.

When he turned round to check out the supercargo, Hocker said gallantly, 'Stone the crows, we've got that green-eyed midget on the trip. Don't sit on that ribbed deck, it'll corrugate your enthusiasm. Sit on my knee. You can toy with my communicator.'

He even held out his hands to lift her over the squab. She leaned forward as though to take up the offer and had his left wrist in a double grip, before he could check that the green eyes were baleful as a hunting cat's.

She said, 'The only reason I do not break off your hand ees that you might be useful. Though I do not know how that could posseebly be.'

160

Adams said, 'Give it him back Xenia. It's just his friendly nature. No offence intended.'

Hocker unable to speak because of pain was making plans as sadistic as any Scotian's. He hunched round in his bucket seat and considered the view.

There was not much of it. Fletcher was swinging the car to line up on a thin illuminated line he had drawn on the miniature chart spread. He had taken the car to its ceiling of two hundred metres. Below, the baked earth was invisible. They could be anywhere, hot as hell and black as the inside of a bag.

He said curtly, 'Seal up. I want all the power there is,' and cut refrigeration.

The car fled on, a hurrying dark capsule, threading an infinity of darkness, silent except for the faint whine of its overdriven motors. After two hours, there was the dubious bonus of more light from one of Garamas's small moons that appeared from dead astern and raced over the desert in a brief, spectacular passage.

The ground below was changing in character. It was more undulating, with occasional patches of grey lichen, where underground features retained a scanty water supply.

Heat levels were falling. Carrick said 'Thirty-nine Celsius,' and the statement coincided with a new onset of darkness as the moon whipped away over the horizon.

Fletcher switched to auto and pulled out the detailed pilotage manual for the quadrant. He said, 'Another hundred kilometres and we meet the outlying farm areas.'

There was a change in the quality of their black shroud. Darkness was thinning out. Fletcher went down to five metres and switched in the sonar beam. Hedge-hopping, the car would be more difficult to pick up. Hablon's military units would be in the area and to be intercepted too far

161

from the headquarters would waste time they did not have.

Now there were lights on the ground. Backwoods Garamasians followed a traditional pattern of sober industry. To bed with the sun and up before sunrise. There was a lot to be said for the ordinary man, he had never been afraid of hard work. He deserved better leadership.

Heat level had dipped to twenty-five Celsius. They stripped off space gear, stacking it methodically on the storage racks. Adams broke out a ration pack and passed nutrient bars to all hands. Released from its confining shell, Xenia's pollen-cloud spread round the set. It had all the earmarks of a picnic on the grass.

When the car stopped and sank on its skids in the shelter of a white, adobe cube, it was difficult to believe that they had reached journey's end without challenge. It was too simple.

Fletcher slid back the hatch and the rhythmic beat of a pump sounded from behind the wall, an isolated heart, pumping in the darkness. He sent up a pencil-slim periscope and infra-red light gave them a picture on the scanner.

A kilometre distant, across a field of blue *erichthoneus*, was the tower block of the commune headquarters; on a bigger scale than any other agricultural admin centre they had seen and surrounded by a pale nimbus of a light from sources on its hidden sides.

The field by-passed the building on the right flank; left a low boundary wall, neatly built of irregular dry stone ran to the corner of the structure, dividing off another production area which was lying fallow and showed up as a spread of yellow ochre corrugation.

It all looked very peaceful.

Xenia said, 'Eet ees decepteeve. All these places have underground access to a monorail circuit. Supplies come een and go out that way.'

162

Movement from the far left made a period. A long olive-drab shuttle, flying a three-ringed pennant appeared briefly and swept out of sight.

Fletcher flicked the eye piece shut and set his periscope to retract. Before it had clicked home in its housing, he knew what he had to do. The invisible courtyard would be stacked with military craft. A small I.G.O. scout car could be shot down before there was any chance to establish its diplomatic mission.

He said, 'Hocker. Get yourself outside. Cut a hole in this wall. Go through and stop the pump.'

Whatever else was going on, there would be a maintenance staff to keep the district working.

Xenia broke her fakir's vigil and climbed over the squab to breathe excitedly down Fletcher's neck. It was a reminder of her physical presence which disturbed his train of thought. He made a conscious effort to exclude her and foraged on the roof rack for a couple of limpet mines which he worked on briefly and then stored in a sling bag.

Hocker using a vibrator from the car's external tool rack, completed his seal hole and heaved himself through. The pump stopped and the silence flowed in like a tangible tide.

Two minutes later, there was the uneven cough of a tractor from across the field.

Carrick said, 'You have to give it to these goons. They run a taut ship.'

There was enough light for the moving shadow to show up on the scanner. The tractor was a light weight spindly structure with huge inflated tyres to roll over the crop without causing damage. It stopped five metres from the pump house and the scene developed like a shadow play.

Two Garamasians jumped down from the high seat, elongated comedy figures. One carried a cranked key, like a winding handle and shoved the business end home in a slot in the wall.

Fletcher had seen enough. He was moving out before the man had completed one revolution. He paused at the breach to set his laser for a wide-angle stun beam and went through in a smooth flow of effort.

The watchers saw the two men stoop to lift the counterweighted door and stop dead as it reached shoulder height. Then Hocker reappeared at the hatch.

'Fletcher says only two can play. You're to hang on here. Rejoin *Petrel* if and when. That includes you, midget. Pass out that sling bag.'

As he took it from Carrick, Xenia was out and standing beside him. Seen full length, she was wearing a metallic belt round her narrow waist with a short narrow bladed knife looped dangerously in an open link.

Hocker said, 'Not you. They'd think we brought the circus.'

The knife was pricking into his throat before he could settle the sling on his shoulder. It was clear enough that she would as soon push it right in as not.

He shrugged and turned away. Why should he sweat. Let Smart-Alec Fletcher sort out his own women. But when he stood again on the floor of the pump house she was nowhere in sight.

He said, 'That little silver bint followed me out. But I reckon she must have thought better of it.'

Fletcher, thinking forward to the enterprise, hardly heard, took the sling bag and ducked under the half-open door.

Climbing to the high bench seat, he was presented with a totally unfamiliar instrumentation spread. The buggy was, however, vibrating quietly, so he had no starting problem. Out from a plain bulkhead under the windshield, two rods curved out to fall naturally to the hands of anyone in the driving seat.

Methodically checking out combinations he tried moving them one at a time and found they would each engage at four angles. It was not until he pulled them both down that there was a soft definitive click and they began to move slowly ahead. Now he could feel free lateral play on the sticks and moved the left hand out. The buggy swung ponderously on its tracks turning right.

Once he had the trick, it was easy. Both down for forward. Left or right fed power to the drive on that side, so that it turned on the slowing wheels and moved contrary to hand shift. He crossed the field in a straight run for the tower wall.

From underneath, it was blank as a cliff. Huge to be so featureless; showing up now as a rectangular mass against faint etiolated bars of pale, blue light.

They slewed away to follow the front, rounded the corner in a controlled spin and trundled on. Precisely in the centre of this frontage an archway led into the thickness of the building as though into a mine.

Fletcher spun the buggy into the entrance and saw fifty metres of oblong section tunnel lit by brilliant roof ports and painted white. No human operator was visible, but as they approached, a maroon and white check barrier lifted like a portcullis.

The buggy was obviously recognised and given official clearance by a scanning eye.

At the end of the run the paved roadway funnelled out to a central courtyard where the architect had used up all the spare libido held back from the stark exterior walls.

The entire floor was paved with red and white squares of ridged tile. In the centre, an oval pool had violent colour patches where *merope* bushes appeared to grow from its indigo surface. Inner walls glowed with translucent brick;

165

ornamented columns decorated with bird beaks ran in colonnades on two sides, a third was set with mammoth standards and an array of banners hung down, still as stonework, crimson and black, bearing the interlaced rings of Garamas and a legend that Fletcher could not read.

On the left, the olive-drab shuttle was drawn up at a semicircular entrance port. On the right, a more utilitarian working area was laid out with parking bays for farm plant. Beyond the pool, a mixed bag of military-design cars was drawn in convoy as though ready for the road, each carrying a pennant with the organization slogan and three luminous, metallic rings.

Fletcher took it all in, with a concentrated pan round the set and swung off to run into an empty slot among the tractors. Dead ahead, through the cloister, a clear window showed a long office spread. A uniformed Garamasian lifted his head from a desk-bound chore, focussed first at wheel level and then looked casually at the driving seat. Puzzled, rather than alarmed, he put down a stylus and began to walk towards the window to get more definition.

Framing a question at mental level, Fletcher got a clear answer from somewhere below his feet. Xenia's voice, as she wriggled free from the angled chassis members where she had hitched a ride, said urgently, 'The operations room ees under the left block. Through that porteeco and down. Below eet, ees the arsenal.

It was useless to make anything of it, certainly he could not send her back, he said, 'We'll never cross the square without challenge.'

The Garamasian had made his mind up. He was back at his desk snatching up a video.

Reading Fletcher's unspoken thought, Xenia went on, 'A diversion. Send a buggee across to crash eento that tidy line. I'll do eet.'

166

She was off like quicksilver, before he could reply. Seconds later, the end tractor coughed into life and backed out of its bay.

Still in reverse, it picked up speed and Xenia dived over its clumsy nose like any Minoan bull leaper. It skirted the pool with wheels overlapping the brink and was beating up to fifteen kilometres an hour as it ploughed into the middle car of the waiting line.

Reaction was immediate and positive. Suddenly, the court-yard was full of high-shouldered Garamasians, all in uniform, all carrying machine carbines.

Movement was all towards the wreck. Fletcher and Hocker crossed at a sprint and met Xenia at the entrance. She was grinning with a girl's simple pleasure, and led without hesitation for a ramp leading down, a silver rabbit on the home run.

Short corridors with right angle turns followed the foundation structure of the block. At the second turn, a Garamasian guard hurrying to answer the call was blasted by Hocker with a yell frozen in his gullet. They left him leaning against a wall with his eye disks rolled up to show pearl grey blanks.

They were running. Footsteps beating a light tattoo on the parquet. Another level down and Xenia panted out, 'Somewhere there weell be a beam barrier.'

The words were still rippling about when Hocker found it. He had gotten a pace ahead and crumpled from the knees with his momentum sliding him forward along the tiled floor.

Fletcher grabbed for Xenia and threw himself back. They went down in a tangle with his arms round her head to keep it from harm. He saw her eyes centimetres from his own, wide and green and full of appreciation. But verbal thanks were never uttered. Black nights filled his eyes. Uniformed figures

167

had swarmed in from all sides through concealed entry ports which had sliced open.

Many hands made light work of carrying them forward to the room they had come to seek. Round the walls, men in green uniforms looked round indifferently before turning again to the winking lights of the sitrep spreads they were serving. Operators, all set to shove magnetized disks on route lines, on a wall-sized operations map, rested on their rakes.

It was left to the select group round the boardroom table in the middle of the floor to take executive action.

Pedasun, standing beside Hablon at the head of the table justifiably pettish at another delay, said, 'Set them in the analyser. Quickly now. There is no time to waste.'

CHAPTER TEN

WHEN his head cleared, convoluted whorls of mist rolling back from a deep black centre, Dag Fletcher first believed he had fetched up in a mortician's parlour.

He was lying in a casket-shaped box, with his neck on a padded rest, on the specimen side of a large lens with the diminished eye of a busy researcher looking in. Ten centimetres from his face, the thick crystal filled the frame from edge to edge. Electrode plates pressing on his temples prevented any forward movement and set up a tension which immediately began to mount to the threshold of destructive pain.

With all its strangeness, it was recognizable enough. One way or another, any technologically advanced culture in the Galaxy had the trick of it. He was hooked to a lay out that could probe into his head, and from the way they were going about it, one of the primitive kind that left a snail-trail of neural damage where it went.

Whatever he had thought, humorous, treacherous, kindly, picayune or full of ultimate truth as an egg would be winkled out and pawed over by Pedasun or some such.

Grimly, he set himself to put out a smoke screen, filling the surface of his mind with pictures. Xenia would do, having a strong emotional overtone. He tried to build an identikit portrait which they could throw on their screen.

Straight, narrow nose, level brows, serious mouth of a voluptuary, small round chin. Profoundly symmetrical like Nature her own self. Proportionate. A number sequence started in his head and he concentrated on developing it. 1. 2. 3. 5. 8. 13. 21. 34. 55. Mathematics of the Golden Section. Silver Section in this case.

A voice in Garamasian penetrated harshly into his private world, followed, from a point left, by Xenia herself saying aloud, 'You are theenking about *me*, Harree, even at thees time. I like that.'

Then the same Garamasian voice, this time using the *lingua franca* of the Galaxy, grated out, 'It is useless to resist, Commander. Your Lieutenant has told us all we need to know. Your ship will not arrive here. A Scotian frigate will intercept it.'

Xenia called out, speaking quickly in English, 'Don't believe anytheeng you hear, I know thees too well.' Her voice cut in an involuntary scream as some linguist used direct action to put in a period.

More Garamasian gobbledegook came from his right side and he felt weight on his feet as the whole container began to move.

From being horizontal, he was tipping forward, pivotting at a point near the waist. Finally, he was upright, more weight on his feet; but a spine-stretching residue still carried by the head harness. Now he could see the operations room through the distorting lens, as though it ran for half a kilometre, with Pedasun diminished to a small bright miniature, standing beside a lifelike, overblown status tricked out with campaign medals and a near conical hat.

The glass screen was swung clear and the two key figures leaped forward, hell bent on joining him in his box. Without the optical filter, he found they stabilised seven metres away, across a shiny table top and the one he had taken to be a lay figure spoke up for the duo. 'Before the operator opens your head, Earthman, I will tell you that you will die. You are a terrorist. You can expect no less.'

Fletcher found his voice feeble in his own ears, when he said, 'I am here as representative of the Inter Galactic Organization. If you have charges to make, your Government will deal with them. Meanwhile, I tell you that your attempt to seize power without a referendum is against the I.G.O. Charter. I formally advise you to use normal political channels for your movement.'

Hablon's teeth showed in a smile which was a mere rictus and had no element of humour in it. Pedasun fidgetted with his cane and looked at his time disc. This was all for the birds, he did not want the old dough-bag sidetracked into a seminar on human rights.

The General, however, had posterity to think of and missed no opportunity to spread the good word. Though logic should have told him he was wasting it on an alien about to be shuffled off. He said, 'I am the Government. Garamas will change. I have no time for neutrality and the I.G.O. milk-and-water constitution. Garamas will be great as she should be. There is not much information that you can give. What there is, I will leave to the Scotian specialists to unravel. We leave now for Kristinobyl. Before we arrive, you at least will be dead.'

Like a hidden theme running behind the words, Fletcher was trying to listen to something else. Then he realised it was not from an outside source. Xenia was whispering urgently from somewhere inside his head. 'Harree, theenk weeth me. Join your mind weeth mine. Theenk about the electrode on your head. Eet uses microvoltages we can match. Concentrate togethaire. Project all your mental energee to that point. Send som surge back up their spout. Theenk weeth me.'

171

Hablon was still going on. Xenia's contribution was interrupted by a quickly choked gasp of pain, which came definitely through normal aural channels. Anger flared redly through his mind. That and feeling for her. She was one on her own. He threw every atom of concentration into willing the current to reverse its flow.

Hablon had stopped and was looking to his left, where Xenia's casket must be. There was a second's dead silence and a movement from the right, where the operator was reaching too late for a balancer to correct the circuit input and stop the blowback along the delicate wiring of the cephalograph.

There was a small plosive plop and an acrid stench of burned-out dielectric. Also, a bonus, which she could not have planned for. The unexpected reversal had tripped more than one relay. The magnetic grips at wrist and ankle had gone slack.

He knew without asking that she was experiencing the same and fairly shouted into her head. 'Out. Together. Over the table.'

There was a confused impression of many heads turning and one guard, quicker off the mark than the rest, whipping a carbine round to aim. Then he dived for the shiny table top and crossed it in a sliding tackle that brought his hands to Hablon's neck.

His back crawled, expecting the hammer thump of an old fashioned slug tearing into its tissue. But the guard had a problem. Killing Hablon with the alien would make him nobody's friend. While he hesitated, the good minute passed. Fletcher had dropped from the table and shifted behind the General with one arm round his throat in a grip that was on the way to lifting off his head.

Over the high shoulder, he saw Hocker, slower off the mark,

stumble from a casket and walk blindly into a Garamasian guard who clubbed him obligingly with the barrel of his carbine. But Xenia was beside him. Her lime green suit had been reduced to fragments which fell away on the trip and long incisions from throat to navel were running with glistening ichor.

In her hand, she now carried her own small knife, stained to the hilt with a greeny-yellow pus.

Leaning against the box she had lately left, a tall Scotian was trying to get an air ration through a severed throat. Reptilian though he was, and a miserly user, it was a losing battle and he was giving up.

When the circuit blew, he had been listening to Hablon and had parked the knife conveniently in a fleshy part of Xenia's shoulder.

Pulling it free and using it in the same movement had been pure therapy to the Fingalnan and she was actually grinning like a pleased cat when she joined Fletcher.

Her knife probing a centimetre into the skin over Hablon's heart was a better argument than Fletcher's neck lock and had the advantage that the man could speak, if he had any worthwhile contribution to make.

She said, 'Tell them to stay where they are or you weell surely die.'

Hablon, far enough on the politician's road to be incapable of giving a direct answer temporized with, 'What can you gain? If you kill me you will die. If you do not, you only delay your death a little time. There is no escape for you.'

It was all true. Fletcher read the resignation in Xenia's mind. She would go on with it. But she expected nothing. The knife, when it left Hablon, would find a billet in her own breast.

The strap of the sling pouch he had carried was beside the

foot of the table and he picked it out as though he had known it was there all the time.

Movement towards them was gradual but definite. The circle was closing. Pedasun's eyes never left Fletcher's face. He would have moved sooner, but he had seen a personal advantage. They had nothing to lose. They were fanatics. They might very well kill Hablon and that would be no bad thing.

Xenia sensed the movement as a mental thing, which she could not see and repeated 'Tell them to stand steell.' At the same time, she shoved the knife a few millimetres nearer its beating goal.

Fletcher had one limpet out and shoved the bag onto the table. He made rapid adjustments on its face and then balanced it flat on his two palms as though holding a thin-shelled egg.

Speaking in the *lingua franca*, so that everyone could judge the situation on its merits, he said, 'I have set this mine for impact detonation. I only have to drop it. Unless I can take it with me, we shall all go up.'

It saved Hablon from any direct veto. He could and did, however, begin to sweat. Higher command was normally on a knoll, unprejudiced by personal discomfort.

Forward movement ground to an uneasy halt. Xenia said nothing, but there was a small surge of optimism on the E.S.P. link. Pedasun, nearest the bomb, took half a pace back.

It was a small gesture, but it set the seal on belief.

Xenia took out her knife and stood clear looking suddenly very tired and small.

Fletcher spoke again into the silence, 'Walk over to the door, Xenia, see if you can get Hocker on his legs. I'll follow you.'

She said, 'I'll try. But frankly you would be better without that one.'

Every eye on the set tracked them as they crossed the floor.

174

Every armed guard had unshipped a carbine and had it aimed at Fletcher's head. He could guess the calculation that was running in each mind. Could any athletic type whip in and catch the mine as it fell?

Pedasun had made the same appreciation and spoke up for prudence. He knew of the magazine under their feet. Sympathetic detonation would send it up. Time, as he judged, was on his side. 'Let them go. They cannot get far. The bomb might just as well go off outside.'

It was the obvious choice. Once in the open, they could be picked off in a safe place.

Xenia was stooping over Hocker, slapping his cheeks with an open hand. When he stirred and sat up she said venomously 'On your feet, Lieutenant. Thees ees no time for lyeeng down. *Queek.*'

He allowed himself to be led away like a dumb beast, shaking his head from side to side, while he tried to clear his eyes of double vision.

In the corridor, they ran a gauntlet of guards drawn up along either wall. But the good word had gone ahead. There was no move to intercept.

As they took the slope of the ramp, Hocker stumbled once against Fletcher's arm and audience participation took a spiral up.

Fletcher steadied the mine and centred it afresh on his extended palms. Xenia said sharply, 'Watch heem. That was suggested to heem. Those treeck boxes have a two-way feed. Maybe they planted some ideas.'

At the portico, Fletcher had knocked up the pace to a jog trot. Without check, he broke into a weaving run. Order had been restored in the square and the leading car in the convoy had been shifted along, until it stood hardly twenty metres off with its entry hatch open.

He was inside with his bomb on the seat and Xenia crawling heroically over the hatch coaming, before the first guards had cleared the archway.

Hocker standing outside said stupidly, 'What's the rush?'

'We have ten seconds to get out.'

'Why?'

'The second mine. It's set to blow anytime now. Get in.'

A racing assessment of the panel, which was more familiar than that of a tractor, and he was moving off.

Hocker was running back. He shouted over his shoulder, 'I have to warn them.'

Xenia stood up with a total mobilization of all the strength she had left, steadying herself with one hand braced against the roof. Her free arm flicked like a whip and Hocker dropped face forward to the tiles with her knife buried to the hilt in his back. Then they were surging for the gatehouse.

A fusillade ripped into the car's fabric and its plexiglass dome fell away in shards.

Ahead, the portcullis closed the way and Fletcher lobbed his bomb forward in an overarm cast that hit it dead centre. At the same, time, he crouched down, one arm pinning Xenia to the squab and slammed in all the power they had.

Blast, funnelling back, tore at the car. Small trash with projectile force hammered through its plating. Flame filled the tunnel with a furnace roar and they hurled themselves for the heart of it.

Momentum carried them through. But the car was a write-off. Automatically fighting the controls, he got level flight for the fifty metres it took to plough itself in a belly dive into the fallow field.

Before it had properly stopped, he was out. Xenia did not move and he climbed back into the smoking wreck to find her.

She lay across his arms, like a sacrifice, streaked with carbon, hair singed and falling straight back from her head.

It was light enough to see the adobe house over the dividing wall and he had crossed three furrows towards it, when a seismographic ripple shook the ground and threw him to his knees.

The long wall undulated like a shaken rope. Still kneeling, he twisted round to look at the building.

Walls were fissured from top to bottom and still moving out. A ragbag of artifacts was spilling from the widening rents. Towards the top, the single figure of a man scrabbled like a beetle at an impossible angle, lost traction and went into free fall. Dust and debris were pluming from the centre in a mushroom cloud.

Fletcher struggled to his feet, but the simple mathematics of it was impossible. Before he could clear the next fifty metres, the section of leaning wall would be spread flat over the area he was in.

The pump house had subsided in a heap of rubble. *Petrel*'s car was running clear and then circling towards him. He tried to wave it back, but it came on.

Carrick had done the sum. There was no time for a stop to take them aboard. He ran past, turned in the narrowing angle of toppling masonry and came up from behind, two metres off the ground.

Fletcher heaved the girl over his shoulder and grabbed for the skids. Then they were airborne, with a jerk that went a fair way to dislocating his arms.

The draught of the falling slab fanned his back. The car's transom was a bare metre from the leading edge. A percussive thump deafened him, so that he could hear nothing and it was only Adams' face hanging upside down from the floor hatch, that gave a visual clue that questions were being asked.

He felt Xenia's weight go from his shoulders. Then Adams was there again, gripping his wrists and helping him to climb aboard.

Carrick said, 'Diplomacy's not for you, Commander. You're a natural born demolition man. For godsake, what did you do in there?'

With a moving deck under his feet, Fletcher could agree with the first element in the proposition. From first to last his intervention on the political scene had brough destruction. From here on in, he would stick to his last. If Varley or anybody at all wanted an *agent provocateur*, they would have to find somebody else.

He had Xenia laid out on the diagonal of the freight bay and was swabbing away the silvery ichor that welled from her incisions. How much blood she had lost, he could not tell. But none of the plasma in the emergency pack would do any good. *Petrel* did not carry Fingalnan blood. Only a major hospital unit in Kristinobyl would have the right setup.

Instant sutures checked any further flow. She was alive, but with what margin, he could not tell.

Carrick spoke again on a different tack which got an answer. 'Something stirring in the heap. Military car coming out.'

Unbelievably, it was true. Rising like a phoenix from the ashes, a long olive-drab shuttle was nosing from the dust pall.

Fletcher thought, 'Good luck to whoever it is. They've beaten the statistics against survival.' Then he recognized the danger. It could be Pedasun or Hablon and the whole scene might be to do over.

He hauled himself across the squabs to the pilot seat, 'Shift across. Adams, get into the bay and see that Xenia doesn't roll about.'

'A pleasure, chief.'

Then he was urging the overworked car to climb to its ceiling in a tight turn that would bring them over the ruins.

Resurrection for the Garamasian shuttle was a hesitant and marginal thing. It had lifted twenty metres from the heart of chaos and was on the brink of failure. Panels stove in, plexiglass dome awry, it was a fugitive from the breaker's yard.

Fletcher had it in his sights and dropped like a stone with the laser carving a bright lance path.

The glowing line sliced along its axis. It stalled, dipped suddenly at the stern and fell away into the smoke. Fletcher pulled out in a climb that settled him back in the bucket seat and rocketed out into bright day. Almost dead ahead, a brilliant fire ball was drifting down into the blue *erichthoneus* field.

Petrel was coming in on a blaze of retro.

Cotgrave said, 'Not another word from I.G.O., Commander. I guess they've clamped right down on Duvorac. That lets us out. I reckon we can't rejoin the squadron.'

The same analysis had gone through Fletcher's head and he was not sure why he hesitated.

Xenia was still out and visibly weakening, a small, silvery toy figure strapped in his own acceleration couch. He could not tell what time she had; but even *Europa*'s sick bay was not fitted for alien medicare.

It could be days before Varley ordered the squadron into Kristinobyl.

She was one factor among many and the book said only a minor one. There was a Scotian over the city. He had no right to hazard the ship for one life. *Europa* could blast the frigate before she was in range of its armament.

179

Decision came at a level below the conscious mind and brought with it a sudden clarification of all the issues as they related to himself. Whether it fitted any external pattern or not, in the last analysis, he was loyal to an individual and no system or institution whatever.

Once sure, he was totally concentrated and single-minded. He switched in the general net and said, 'Commander to all stations. The Fingalnan girl will die, unless we can get her to Kristinobyl. There's a Scotian blocking the vector, which has to be shifted anyway in due course. I'm going to try. But I need a navigator, an engineer, a communicator and a gunner. The rest can take the car and go overland, hole up near the city and wait for the squadron. Press clearance tabs if you join me.'

There was a count of three and he swivelled slowly, keeping his eyes off the co-pilot's console, where the indicator lights would show up.

Cotgrave said formally, 'Co-Pilot to Commander. All systems go. Ready when you are.' Only then, he looked across and saw the full bank of affirmative signals.

Fletcher said simply, 'Thank you all hands. Count down as of now,' and began feeding course data to the main computer.

There was no doubt in his mind that as soon as he had cleared the ground by a kilometre, the Scotian would have him pinpointed. It was all a matter of how soon he recognized a threat and broke station. There would be a debate going on in the commander's head. If he had been told to sit over Kristinobyl, he might first try to get the order cancelled. Only a crystal ball would reach Pedasun or Hablon. Eventually, he would use his own initiative. It all depended on what that was.

That much was abundantly clear to Toron in *Alope*'s

crowded control cabin. Already, the unusual seismographic shock waves registered in the Velchanos area had put him on alert. As *Petrel* showed on the scanner, action stations sounded through the ship. He beamed once on the private link for Pedasun and raised only a waiting call. Intuiton told him that the organization below was all to hell. Somebody should have known. Somebody should have been calling him with the score.

Petrel jacked herself another ten kilometres into the gravis-phere and Toron moved, calling for a course change that put his reptilian crew on the edge of G tolerance.

The move was repeated on *Petrel*'s scanner. Fletcher had expected it and broke the auto chain. Working on manual, with his own fallible human computer, he reckoned he could offset the frigate's heavier weight in instrumentation.

Alope blazed through the space they should have been in with her main armament cutting a swathe that would have dissipated *Petrel* in incandescent gas and Fletcher was fighting a spiral that strained every seam in the corvette's hull.

Alope had checked, lizard-quick and was coming round for another run.

Fletcher called for retro and the corvette's deceleration blacked half the crew. He asked, thickly, for Carrick, in his fire control, and got a burst of welcome profanity that showed the marine was still operational.

Alope's dive, which should have given her cone a long sight along the corvette's spine, had taken her down steeply almost dead ahead.

Fletcher, reduced to a living extension of the machine under his hand, was on to it knowing that it was his chance and that it was, in all likelihood, the only one he would get.

He flung *Petrel* after the diving frigate, with motors in a howl, as power went into the red quadrant for overload.

Petrel came in like a projectile fired at a standing butt, with the three rings of *Alope*'s jacks widening as if in a zoom lens.

They were solid, black spiked rocks to shatter the corvette. Then they were splayed out, fragments in an exploded diagram, and Fletcher was clawing for sea room to avoid the main wreck, ploughing through a penumbra of fist-sized trash.

Damage control lights were winking on every console, *Petrel* was a sieve with collision bulkheads dropping in every module.

Fletcher had time to think that he had killed Xenia anyway, then he was manoeuvring to dive for Kristinobyl's space port. There was still another and if he let her get into the sky it could only end one way.

He took *Idron* at her most defenceless. Her commander had belatedly realised that *Alope* needed help against the corvette. She was a hundred metres from the pad, still blind in wreathing flame, when Carrick raked into the narrow waist and settled her back in two broken cylinders that rolled in flaming cartwheels among the blast trenches.

Petrel blazed down on her old station. Grey coolant jetted out for a military planetfall. Before the gas had cleared, Carrick and his marines were out as a bridgehead, facing every quarter, with heavy calibre lasers at the aim.

Fletcher was calling the terminal. 'I.G.O. command. Hear this. Any offensive action will be met by total devastation. Send out a hospital tender. Alert Kristinobyl General for Fingalnan casualty. Priority One.'

He took her in the tender himself, feeling her cold to the touch and knowing that he could be already too late.

To Cotgrave, he said, 'Accept no orders from anyone. Not me. Not anyone. Blast anything that moves within a hundred metres of the ship. Signal Varley and tell him you are standing by.'

The streets of Kristinobyl were almost deserted and strewn with debris, as the tender swept through with two outriders, wailing their sirens in an unnecessary warning to traffic which was not there.

The hospital itself was busy enough, with a log jam of patient Garamasians waiting for attention at the street accident units. Black obsidian eye discs turned incuriously to follow him as he walked beside a wheeled trolley into reception. Whatever else, the xenophobic phase had burned itself out. Most looked bewildered, as though they had wakened from a confusing dream.

When he left her, with a full set of six doctors, fourteen nurses and an engineer to run an emergency power system, he felt suddenly out of programme. The heavy duty laser he had carried as additional argument was incongruous and he shoved it back in its clip. He paced about the small ante room to the theatre, knowing that if he stopped or sat down he would have to give in to sleep.

A half hour passed and there was no movement from the closed door. Once he had thought he could hear her trying to say something, then it was gone.

A Garamasian orderly wheeled in a trolley with coffee and sandwiches and he realized it was a long time since he had eaten any food.

Then there was the noise of several feet in the corridor and a muffled argument in gobbledgook as though the medical staff were putting up a protest.

When the outer door sliced back, he expected a posse—remnants of Pedasun's crew still acting out their brief. He stood balanced on the balls of his feet, willing up a reserve of energy. There was some truth in the old gag that those who lived by the sword perished by it. There was never a point in a vendetta when both parties were ready to call quits at the same time. But it was Yola with Termeron and an elderly mandarin type, dressed in an expensive-looking caftan with a round collar and a broad electrum belt.

Yola said, 'We guessed it was you. I have brought my father, Kaalba, to meet you. There is no need to threaten the city with your ship. He is anxious to talk with you; but I must translate for him.'

Taken at one remove, Fletcher had time to study the Provincial Governor's face, while he spoke and even before he had the meaning, he had judged that the man was sincere. Relayed by Yola in English, it came down to a policy statement that would please Duvorac for one, if he was still batting. The recent events had made it clear to senior citizens of all parties that government could not be left in the hands of politicians. A new National Front was proposed with good men of every party called in. Purposeful work and a programme of reform was to be the keynote. There was plenty to do and Garamasian traditional virtues were strongest when there was a hard furrow to plough. The abortive revolution had been a timely warning. He was thanked for his part in crushing it in time. Nothing was said of the sabotage to the ring.

But Yola herself was not entirely at ease. She at least suspected the truth, but was, maybe, prepared to list it as the ill wind and suspend judgement.

When they had gone, he sat down. There was no immediate threat. Tension had gone out of the situation.

How much later he could not say, there was a hand shaking his shoulder and a Raggedy-Ann in a white smock leaning over the chair. Outside it was dark and the hospital's emergency lighting left a lot of shadow. The blaster was out and jabbing for the shroud before he was fully orientated and the nurse leaped back a full pace with a startled 'Eek.'

184

Vision clearing, he said thickly, 'Sorry about that. How is she?'

'You can see her for two minutes. Follow me.'

They must have wheeled her out while he was asleep. There was a short corridor to traverse and then a pause outside a door, before he was ushered through into a large room with panoramic windows showing like a dark star map.

Xenia was lying flat on a high bed and turned her head to follow him in, a small silver nude under a clear plexiglass dome. Her voice spoke directly into his head with the text pointed by brilliant green eyes, almost all pupil, '*Harree,* I have to stay here, *five* days. Then you weel be gone. But eet does not mattaire, does eet? I shall always remembaire you. Weell you theenk about me?'

She had accepted that they would go different ways. Now he knew that it was so. For as long as they held together in a human shell, they would be part of the texture of each other's minds. But there was no ongoing future for them in any part of the Galaxy.

He projected back. 'No, it does not matter. Yes, I shall always think about you. Relax, everything has turned out well. I'll be in again to see you.'

Then the nurse was saying, 'Time to go, Commander, she must not be over tired.'

Dag Fletcher had one more call to make, before he could return to his ship and set about a repair schedule. A V.I.P. shuttle took him to the I.G.O. complex and he found Duvorac sitting in his office as though he had not moved since the last call. He was looking greyer than ever under the temporary power supply and spoke in carefully husbanded bursts of energy.

'Commander. You have done well. The situation has stabilized. We can look forward to better days on Garamas. Your part will not be forgotten. I have spoken with your Admiral. He agrees with me that it would be tactless to bring the squadron in immediately. Give them time to organize. You are to stay here. Four weeks to prepare your ship. You are confirmed in command of *Petrel*. The enquiry has come out with commendation for your conduct in the *Terrapin* affair. For the time being, you are the I.G.O. Military Adviser for this sector. I hope I do not need to apply to you. Any questions?'

'Only one. What is to happen to the Fingalnan agent?'

'Xenia? When she is fit to travel, say in a month's time, she will return to I.G.O. H.Q. for leave and later a new briefing.'

Riding back to his ship, Fletcher recognised her mind penetrating the night to speak to him. Tenuous at this distance, it was no more than an earnest of infinite good will, a frail human gesture, at this instant of time, against the cosmic backdrop of uncertainty.

Time anyway was still on their side. They had a month. When rightly considered, that was as far as any man would wish to see into the future.

He sent back as a signal, the single all-embracing service word for acceptance of the logic of any situation.

'Check.'